The Carnival of the Animals

The Carnival Of The Animals

By
Elizabeth Varadan

Illustrated By
Peter and Susan Fraser

Belanger Books
2018

This book is for my husband, Rajan

Table of Contents

Camille's Dream

Once upon a musical score, Camille Saint-Saëns was stumped. He was composing a piece of music to entertain his friends. An idea twinkled in his mind. A musical fantasy. Animals in a parade.

A tune beckoned. Camille inked in some quarter notes. The melody slipped away.

I must let this idea bloom, Camille thought.

He sat in the stuffed chair by the door and closed his eyes. Music and pictures swirled in his head: A tortoise waltzed. A peacock called. A lion stomped into a forest.

Soon Camille was fast asleep. He dreamed of animals in the zoo. He dreamed of animals far away.

Once upon a time, he dreamed...

King of Beasts

"Here you see Elroi the Lion, King of Beasts."

Once upon a traveling circus, a lion named Elroi gazed out the bars of his cage. The circus had stopped at another small French village where, he knew, a new audience would laugh at him.

I must be the saddest lion in the world, Elroi thought. He had been in Monsieur Basset's Traveling Circus ever since he was a small cub.

If only I could run away. He wished this every night.

The circus wagons were on one side of the village square. Villagers thronged along the other sides to watch the acts. First, Yves juggled his fire sticks. People gasped each time the torches flared into the air. Next, Mignon the Acrobat did backbends and twists. She crossed her ankles under her chin, walking on her hands, and then crossed her ankles behind her neck.

Then Algernon played his barrel organ, his long mustaches jiggling as he nodded his head back and forth. His two golden poodles twirled on hind legs, yipping to the music, which drew delighted laughter from the crowd. Elroi shuddered. Soon he would have to do his tricks.

Too quickly the music ended. Everything grew quiet. Algernon took the dogs to his wagon. The villagers waited. Men scuffed the cobbled ground with restless feet. A boy's voice piped, "Papa, what's next?" A woman straightened the ruffles of her daughter's pinafore before smoothing her own long skirt.

Monsieur Basset opened the side door of the cage and tugged on the rope around Elroi's neck. As Elroi hopped to the ground, an excited "Ooohhh" ran through the crowd. Monsieur Basset led him onto the square. Elroi lashed his tail from side to side, trying to look wild and fearsome.

Monsieur Basset straightened his red jacket and grinned. "Ladies and gentlemen . . ." He pointed a long thin baton at Elroi. "Here you see Elroi the Lion, King of Beasts! This ferocious animal was captured in a jungle only a month ago. But, under my training, he is as harmless as a kitten." He jerked on Elroi's rope, commanding, "Leap over this baton."

Elroi leaped once. He leaped twice. Back and forth he went, three times. The villagers clapped every time.

"Show them how you fight with the air," Monsieur Basset ordered.

Elroi stood up on his back legs and batted his front paws, pretending to box. Everyone laughed.

Then Elroi had to roll over and play dead.

"Roar for them, Elroi," said Monsieur Bassett. "Show them you are the King of Beasts."

Elroi hated this part. He roared. Someone in the crowd roared back. It happened every time, along with more laughter.

Monsieur Basset cocked his head to one side, looking pleased.

Now it was time for Elroi's new trick, which Elroi hated even more than the roar.

"Smile, Elroi," Monsieur Bassett commanded.

Elroi stretched his mouth the way Monsieur Bassett had taught him, revealing all his teeth.

"Someone should pull that lion's fangs," a woman called out. She clutched her small son's arm. "He's dangerous!"

Elroi stopped smiling.

"He could bite someone," a man in leather breeches agreed. He shook a finger at Monsieur Basset. "You could be arrested, Monsieur." Other voices began to mutter.

People shifted from foot to foot. One mother grabbed her toddler and started walking away.

Monsieur Basset put his hands to his head. "Arrested! Non, non, non!" He held his hands out. "I, too, have noticed Elroi is growing more . . . risky, shall we say? I have already planned to have his fangs removed next week," he assured the man.

After the villagers went home, Elroi lay in the darkness, growling and weeping by turns. It wasn't fair. He had done his best for Monsieur Basset, and now he was going to lose his teeth. Why couldn't they just skip the smiling trick? They would have to anyway if his teeth were gone.

Maybe Monsieur Basset just said that, Elroi thought.

But what if he meant it?

Elroi rose and padded to the cage door that Monsieur Basset padlocked each night. He reached a paw around the last bar. It had become his nightly habit. The padlock was in place, cool and hard to his touch. As usual, Elroi pressed his paw against the curved metal loop hooking in the latch. For the first time, the bottom part of the padlock swung free.

Elroi remembered then: Usually there was a clicking sound when Monsieur Basset locked his cage. Tonight, there was no click. Monsieur Basset had grown careless. Elroi's wish had come true. He could run away!

His thoughts raced. He should get rid of the rope on his neck before leaving. He clawed and pulled and gnawed. After some time, the last bits of rope dropped to the cage floor. How good it felt not to have that tight feeling against his throat!

He looked around his cage for the last time—the only home he'd ever known. Now that he could go, questions pressed in on him: How would he find food? Where would he sleep? Maybe he was foolish to think of leaving.

"Life isn't so bad," he whispered. Mignon and Yves always had a kind word for him when they passed his cage. Algernon sometimes sang songs to him when Elroi moped against the bars of the cage.

Elroi shook his shaggy mane. "What am I thinking? Songs and kind words are fine, but not worth losing my teeth. I must be brave and go."

Elroi lifted the padlock with one claw and heard it fall to the ground with a soft plop. He pushed the door slowly open. He leaped to the ground with a faint thud and held his breath. "Goodbye, everyone," he growled softly, and he padded away into the starlit night.

A full moon silvered the cobbled street as he crept through winding lanes leading to a dusty road. Then he loped until he had left the village far behind. Cool air streamed through his mane as he ran past moonlit meadows and stands of trees. How pleasant the clods of dirt felt under his feet. He slowed his steps to enjoy the silvery scene around him.

"Help!" a voice called. Elroi turned and saw a spreading oak tree a few feet away from the road. To his horror, under the tree a fox held a struggling hare in its jaws.

"Help," cried the hare again, but Elroi crouched in the grass, trembling. In his cage, he had often heard conversations between villagers. Foxes were dangerous. They had teeth and claws too.

As Elroi crouched below the tree considering this, a squirrel shifted on a branch above him. An acorn fell on Elroi's head, and he let out a roar of surprise. The fox dropped the hare and bounded away.

"Your roar scared the fox and saved my life," said the grateful hare. "How can I thank you?" He brushed himself off and sat up, his long ears quivering. "How did you happen to be here?"

Elroi told the hare his story.

"Hmm," said the hare. "I can't repay you with anything except advice. Monsieur Bassett will be looking for you. You must run down the road until you come to a large forest. If you hide there, no one can find you."

Elroi thanked the hare and went on his way. The moon was higher, shining its soft light on grasses and limbs of trees. Elroi passed farmhouses and pastures. Finally, tired and thirsty, he stopped at a small stream winding its way through a small copse of poplar trees near the edge of the road.

As he began to lap water, a rustling sound from above made him look up. A large feathered shape swooped down behind him. Elroi turned in time to see a mole disappear into a hole in the ground, while a huge owl stood at the opening, beating its wings, its talons fastened on the mole's tail. The owl turned to glare at Elroi.

Elroi swallowed. He was used to friendly circus dogs. This owl was a hunter. What if it attacked him? Then Elroi thought of the fox, and the way his roar had frightened it off. He opened his mouth wide and gave the loudest roar he could. With a startled screech, the owl released the mole's tail and flew away.

The mole came out of her burrow. "Your roar scared the owl away," she said. "Thanks to you, my babies and I are safe. How can I repay you?"

"I was happy to help," Elroi assured her. His chest swelled with pride. Twice he had frightened a dangerous

21

beast and saved a life. But he still needed to find the forest and hide. Quickly he told the mole his story.

"Ah, the Bouconne Forest," she said. "Keep going along the road and you'll be there before sunrise."

Elroi bade her goodbye and continued his journey. The muscles in his legs rippled as he ran under the star-filled sky. Soon the stream was far behind him. After a while sky began to turn a mysterious deep blue. Far away, the black outlines of trees made shaggy patterns against the horizon. So many trees! Elroi thought. He hoped that was the Bouconne Forest.

A sudden scream made Elroi halt and turn and look at the grass by the side of the road. A hulking badger was snarling at a hedgehog whose needle-like fur stood on end. The hedgehog screamed again as the badger waddled closer.

Without even thinking, Elroi opened his mouth and roared. The badger, hissing and snarling, ran off into a thicket of bushes. Elroi loped over to the frightened hedgehog.

"Your roar saved me," said the hedgehog. "I came out of my burrow to look for food, and there he was! How can I thank you?"

"I'm looking for the Bouconne Forest," Elroi explained, and he quickly told the hedgehog why.

"You're almost there," the hedgehog assured him.

22

Elroi returned to the road and set off once again.

When he reached the edge of the forest, he paused. Oaks and pines and chestnut trees spread before him in shadowed greens.

My new home, he thought. He wondered what he would find. Gone were circus tricks and commands. Gone was the scornful laughter of villagers. What would take their place?

Warily, Elroi entered. Trees closed around him with their spicy leaf scents. Eyes peered from tree hollows. Birds twittered overhead. Squirrels chattered.

Suddenly an owl swooped down, blocking his way. It glared at Elroi, and raised a claw, flexing its talons, demanding, "Who-who-who are you?"

A fox crept up and bared its teeth at Elroi, and said, "We don't want any strangers here!"

A badger waddled close, lowered its long, flat head, and snarled.

Elroi halted. He stared at the owl's talons. He stared at the fox's teeth. He stared at the badger's clawed feet. Remembering his earlier encounters, Elroi drew himself up and took a deep breath. He closed his eyes and threw back his head, letting out a mighty roar that echoed all through the woods. When he looked again, the owl, the fox, and the badger had vanished.

Regal pride filled Elroi's chest as he stalked into the forest. The King of Beasts had arrived.

Who Makes the Sun Rise?

The horse thought. "Go and see the old woman called La Gran-mère," he said.

Once upon a farm in Provence, there lived three foolish roosters, each of whom thought his crowing made the sun come up. Every morning the three cocks would run across the yard with a shrill cry. Then the sun would slowly peep over the far hills, sending rays of golden light into the new day.

"See what I have done!" Marmion would boast. "I may be small, but I have the loudest voice."

"The sun doesn't care about loudness," Bayard would say. "It is my high, pure voice that calls it into the sky."

"You are both wrong," Raoul would scoff. "The sun rises for me, for I have the deepest voice of all."

Then they would each crow again and again, louder and higher and deeper, to prove their point.

One morning their bickering and boasting was angrier than usual. Farmer Bontecou came to the window

27

with his wife and shouted, "Silence!" He turned to his wife and said, "If they don't stop that racket, I'll eat two of them and just keep the one!"

The roosters were too busy crowing to hear, but the farmer's threat frightened their wives. Immediately the three hens gathered together, trying to think of a plan.

"I'll be too upset to lay a single egg if Farmer Bontecou eats Marmion," cried Minette.

"We must do something about their bickering and boasting," said Belle. She put a wingtip to her beak. "Maybe we should tell them we won't talk to them again until they get along."

Each went to her husband and threatened to stop speaking until all the bickering stopped. For the rest of the morning, the hens kept their promise. But the roosters didn't seem to notice.

That afternoon, the hens came together again.

"Not clucking is killing me," said Belle.

"This is harder on us than on them," Reine agreed.

"We should ask the other animals for advice," suggested Minette.

They went to the milk cow.

"All that bickering and boasting upsets me, too," said the cow. She swished her tail. "If they keep it up, it will curdle my milk. Then what good will I be to Farmer Bontecou?"

"What's your advice?" asked Reine.

"Tie some string around their beaks, each night. In the morning, untie only one and let him crow." The cow smiled, pleased with herself.

Belle sighed. "Bayard will untie it right away. He's good with knots."

"So is Marmion," said Minette.

"Raoul is too," said Reine.

The cow frowned. "Maybe you should ask the ram."

The three hens went to the ram.

"All that bickering and boasting upsets me too," the ram said. "If they keep it up, it's going to straighten my wool. Then what good will I be to Farmer Bontecou?"

"What's your advice?" asked Belle.

"We can all use some of my wool to plug our ears every morning."

The three hens stared at him.

"Who will plug Farmer Bontecou's ears?" Minette finally asked.

The ram frowned. "Maybe you should ask the plow horse."

The three hens went to the plow horse.

"All that bickering and boasting upsets me too," said the horse. He gave an impatient toss of his mane. "If they keep it up, it's going to break my eardrums, and I won't hear what I'm told to do. Then what good will I be to Farmer Bontecou?"

"What is your advice?" asked Reine.

The horse thought. "Go and see the old woman called La Gran-mère. She lives down the road in a small hut under a huge apple tree at the end of a crooked path. I've heard Farmer Bontecou's wife say La Gran-mère has cures for many things. Maybe she can cure your husbands of their quarreling."

The three hens set off down the road until they saw the huge apple tree at the end of a crooked path. Sure enough, under the tree was the small hut. Herbs grew near the door and in clumps along the wall. Their pungent scents floated up the path. When the hens reached the door, Reine picked up a stone with her foot and used it to knock.

An ancient wrinkled woman came to the door. She peered at them from milky blue eyes that swirled with secrets.

"Please, Madame, are you La Gran-mère?" asked Minette.

The old woman nodded.

"Can you help us?" asked Belle.

30

"What do you wish?" asked La Gran-mère.

"Our husbands quarrel every morning," Reine told her. "Each one thinks it is his crowing that makes the sun come up."

"Their bickering upsets everyone on the farm," Belle said.

"Farmer Bontecou has threatened to eat two of them if it doesn't stop," said Minette.

"What foolish roosters," the woman exclaimed. "The sun will come up whether they crow or not."

The hens looked at each other in surprise.

"Those roosters have no effect on the sun," said the old woman. "It's the sun that makes them want to crow."

"We just want them to stop bickering, so that Farmer Bontecou won't eat any of them," said Belle.

La Gran-mère smiled. "I can help you teach these foolish roosters a lesson." She went to a shelf and took down a bottle. "This is a sleeping potion," she explained, as she took three pieces of cloth and poured a little of the contents on each cloth.

"Hold these carefully in your beaks," she told them. The three hens nodded.

"When you get home," said La Gran-mère, "each of you rub a kernel of corn with your cloth. Tonight, just before sundown, give each husband a kernel. Tomorrow

31

they will all sleep a little later than usual, and you will see what you will see."

The hens were so grateful, they each laid an egg in payment. Then they rushed back to the farm, where they followed the old woman's instructions and waited.

At last evening came. The sky turned orange and red, then faded into purple and dusky blue. Minette took her cloth to Marmion.

"I'm sorry for scolding you this morning," she said sweetly. "I've brought you a present." She carefully unwrapped the corn with one foot and watched Marmion gobble down the kernel.

"I shouldn't have been cross with you this morning," Belle told Bayard. "Here is a little present to show how sorry I am."

"What a good wife," said Bayard as he ate the corn.

"How thoughtful," said Raoul, taking the kernel Reine offered him.

Then all three roosters fell into a deep sleep. Their wives tiptoed to a corner of the henhouse.

"What if the sun doesn't come up when they don't crow?" Minette whispered.

"La Gran-mère said the sun makes them crow and not the other way around," Reine reminded her.

"But, what if she's wrong?"

"La Gran-mère must know," said Belle. She shivered. "We'll have to wait and see."

The next morning the roosters were still asleep when the first faint rosy light showed over the far hills. Soon the arc of the sun appeared, and its golden light began to warm the sky.

In the strange silence of the morning, the hens and the cow, the ram and the horse, all began to wake, one by one.

"It's first light," said Minette in a hushed voice.

The other hens echoed her, and then the other farmyard animals:

"It's first light."

"First light."

"First light."

Farmer Bontecou and his wife came to the window and looked out.

"What is this?" cried the farmer. "It's morning and I must be about my chores!" He hurriedly dressed, then rushed out under the morning sky to milk the cow and feed the sheep and hook up the horse's plow.

As he ran by the henhouse he peered in and called to the roosters, "What is the matter with you? I count on you every day to get me up!"

His voice awakened the roosters. Once awake, they felt the sun's magic and ran outside to crow loudly at the day.

They stopped and stared at each other.

"The sun is already up!" said Marmion.

"It came up by itself," whispered Raoul.

"Without us," said Bayard.

The three roosters hung their heads in embarrassment.

From then on, when morning came, the roosters still crowed, for they had to obey the sun. Then they went about their business, pecking at corn and scratching for worms. There was never any bickering or boasting again for the rest of their days.

Farmer Bontecou and his wife and the farmyard animals enjoyed the peace and quiet. The three hens were happy, too.

"It was worth an egg," said Minette.

Belle nodded.

"I agree," said Reine. And they all fluffed their feathers and clucked.

Run Like the Wind

Bulging red eyes glared down at Omar. Huge blue lips bared sharp yellow fangs.

Once upon the Syrian Desert, a baby hémione, or wild donkey, named Omar munched a clump of grass. His mother grazed nearby, along with his cousins and Uncle Rashad. All was peaceful on the windswept stony land, when suddenly the ground trembled.

"Hunters!" whispered Omar's mother, sending an arrow of fear through him. Hunters had killed his father and aunt.

Uncle Rashad laid his long ears back. His brushy tail stiffened in warning. "Run!" he brayed to the other wild donkeys. He set off across the rocky steppe desert and the others followed. Omar galloped as fast as he could, but soon he fell behind.

Ahead of him, his mother screamed, "Run, Omar!"

"Run like the wind," shouted Uncle Rashad.

With his young legs, Omar could only run like a little puff of air. Looking over his shoulder, he saw the hunters on horseback drawing closer. Their robes streamed behind them. They waved bows and arrows and urged their horses with terrifying yells.

Omar saw a large bush to his right. "Perhaps I can hide behind it," he told himself.

Just then, a man's voice floated over the bush.

"Swift and lovely hémione beast, you will not be hunter's feast. But you must go farther west long before you safely rest."

To Omar's astonishment, the bush grew larger. Its branches pulled apart and became new bushes. These parted into more bushes. Soon he was looking at a forest of tall shrubs. He dashed inside and the hunters swept by as if he and the forest were invisible.

Coming to a small clearing, Omar saw an old man sitting by a tent in front of a small fire. The man was eating a piece of flat bread. He wore a long white robe. A white turban was wrapped around his head.

"Welcome, young hémione," he said, brushing crumbs from his flowing white beard. "I am Hadi, a soothsayer."

"Soothsayer?" asked Omar, his heart still beating fast.

"I tell fortunes," Hadi said. "I understand the language of animals." He waved a hand at the tall shrubs. "I do other things, too. Come . . ." He patted the ground beside him. "Let me look into your eyes."

Omar obeyed.

"Ah," said Hadi. "Your ancestors once pulled the chariots of kings."

"Yes," said Omar, for Uncle Rashad had told him this.

"And now you are all hunted for meat."

So that was what happened after hunters killed wild donkeys! They ate them! Omar's heart iced over with fear. He drew closer to the fire.

"Listen," said Hadi. "The hunters will be back for you. Soon this magic forest will fade. You must go far away from here."

Omar thought of his mother and Uncle Rashad and his older cousins. A lump of sorrow swelled inside his ribs. "Must I leave my family?"

Hadi said, "Think how sad they will be if you are killed by the hunters."

39

"Can't they come with me?"

"Alas, they didn't hear me calling. You did."

Omar lowered his head. "I can't run fast. That's why."

"They would want you to be safe," Hadi said.

Omar nodded sadly.

"I will summon a jinni," Hadi told him. "If you can be brave, think fast, and tell the truth, he'll help you. If not, he'll eat you himself. Are you able to do these things?"

"I th-th-think so," said Omar.

At that moment, hooves thundered beyond the magic bushes—the hunters returning with their kill. Omar shuddered, wondering who they were taking home to eat. The hooves slowed to a clip-clop.

One hunter called to his friends, "Where is that little one we saw earlier? He'll be a tender mouthful!" The others laughed. Omar gasped.

Hadi rose and took a small copper bottle from under the turban on his head. He looked kindly at Omar. "Let thoughts of your family support you," he said. Closing his eyes, he chanted, "Come, oh servant; serve me true. I have a noble task for you."

He pulled out the bottle's shiny stopper. Thick smoke drifted out of the bottle, floating and billowing higher and rumbling like thunder. When it cleared, Omar saw a giant so tall he had to bend his head back to see the jinni's face.

And what a face it was! Bulging red eyes glared down at Omar. Huge blue lips bared sharp yellow fangs. Omar shuddered.

"Welcome, Jinni," Hadi told the giant.

The jinni touched his many-colored turban and bowed to Hadi. "Sire, I am here," he growled. "What is my noble task?"

Hadi patted Omar's mane. "Help this donkey go far away, over land and sea, and keep him safe from hunters."

The jinni folded arms the size of horses. "Is this miserable piece of donkey flesh worthy of such trouble?" he demanded. "Is he brave? Can he think fast? Does he tell the truth?"

"You may test him yourself," said Hadi. He leaned over and whispered in Omar's ear, "Think of your family and take heart."

Omar forced himself to stare back at the jinni. He made himself raise his ears and stiffen his legs and tail as he had seen Uncle Rashad do when facing danger.

The jinni smiled, as if amused. "Here is your first test," he rumbled. "You cannot cross the sea with hooves that run on desert. How will you make such a journey?"

After a moment's thought, Omar said, "Clouds move across the sky. If I have hooves that can climb clouds, I can follow the clouds across the sea. I've never seen a sea," he added, politely, "but it can't be very big."

The jinni gave a roar that shook the air. "I will give you such hooves," he said, when he finished laughing. "But I promise there are waters bigger than this desert." He bent down, puckered his lips, and sent a stream of air like a desert breeze along Omar's feet.

Beyond the magic forest, the hunters were quarreling.

"I heard thunder; let's go home."

"No, I won't give up."

"He's around here somewhere."

"Here is your second test," the jinni told Omar. "If you climb clouds, the hunters can see your brownish-gray legs, your dark mane, and the black tip of your tail. How will you escape their arrows?"

Omar looked down at his legs, then back at the jinni. "If I am the color of the clouds, arrows won't find me."

The jinni rested fists like camel humps on his hips and eyed Omar. "You will be much changed, little one. No longer a creature of the desert."

Omar thought again of how sad his family would be if the hunters killed him. He looked into the jinni's red eyes.

"I will change only enough to stay alive," he said. "In my heart, I will always be a wild donkey. In dreams, I will gallop this desert with my family. In memory, I will return to this forest to thank you for your kindness."

A glow of approval came into the jinni's eyes. "Sire," he told Hadi. "This young donkey pleases me." He blew a new stream of air over Omar. When Omar looked down, his legs were as white as cloud smear. He looked over his shoulder. His whole body was creamy white.

In a softer voice the jinni said, "There will be no third test. Instead, I give you something to protect your dreams and memories." With a fingernail the size of a donkey's ear, the jinni touched Omar's forehead.

Omar felt a tingle above his eyes. Looking up, he saw a long ivory horn had grown from his forehead.

Then, before his eyes, the magic shrubs began to fade. As if through a green mist, Omar saw the outlines of three hunters on horseback still looking this way and that.

The jinni pulled a cloud from the sky and held it at Omar's feet. "Go," he said.

Omar leaped onto the cloud.

Below, Hadi's voice said, "Well done, jinni! Now we must go, too." A thundering boom made Omar look down. Dark mist floated out of the bottle in Hadi's hands, covered the jinni, and swirled back into the bottle. The jinni was gone.

Light flashed next, and Omar blinked. When he looked again, Hadi was gone. The tent was gone. So were the fire and the magical shrub forest! There were only three surprised hunters sitting on their horses, staring up at Omar.

The tallest one squinted. "Is that a . . . cloud?"

Like a sigh on a breeze, Hadi's voice whispered in Omar's ear: "Run, Omar. Run like the wind."

Omar leaped to a higher cloud, then a higher one. Soon he was running along a misty path that stretched endlessly before him. On and on he ran across the cool clouds. It felt like he was running forever. Above him, the sky turned again and again from the blue of day to the star-sparkle of night. Occasionally Omar stopped to drink fog puddles or nibble cloud tufts. Once he peered down through the mist at a stretch of water so huge he could see no end to it.

"The sea," he whispered. He thought he heard the jinni's rumbling laugh and Hadi's soft chuckle before he set off running again.

At last the path came to an end over a vast green forest. Drifting down through fog wisps, Omar stared in wonder at so many plants: Leaves covered tall spreading trees; grass blanketed the ground; ferns fringed a small pool. Birds peeped. As Omar's hooves lit on the soft ground, a rabbit peered out of its hole.

"Welcome to the Backmuir Wood wondrous creature," it said. Omar touched his horn to the ground in greeting. His new life had begun.

Time passed. Omar grew used to the abundant grass, the chorus of bird song, and small burrowing creatures became his friends. Then one day a family of humans came walking in the woods. Their voices were soft, filled with laughter, and one made strange, wailing music from something he carried and blew into, but Omar remembered the hunters. He fled deep into the woods and hid until the family left.

For the rest of his life, the very sight of humans made Omar flee. Over time, legends grew up, told by the few people who caught a glimpse of him running through the forest—legends of a ghostly white unicorn that could run like the wind.

Each night, Omar returned in dreams to his desert home. Again, his feet touched the rocky soil of the steppe. Again, his dark mane streamed behind him. Again, his mother and uncle and cousins ran beside him. And all of them ran like the wind.

Perchance to Dance

Again, she heard the music and saw Carolina dance her beautiful flower dance.

Once upon a hillside near Provence, a tortoise named Nadine lay on her special rock. She stuck out all four of her thick legs to soak up the sun's warmth. I love spring mornings, she thought. She wiggled her short, pointed tail and curled her claws against the stony surface.

A clatter and the sound of neighing horses from the road below made Nadine raise her smooth head. She crawled to the edge of her rock and looked down. A carriage pulled by two black horses had stopped at the bottom of the slope. A man wearing a tall hat stepped down from the driver's seat and tied the horses to a tree. A woman and two children watched from the carriage window.

Another family on a picnic, Nadine decided. People often came in springtime to climb the hill and eat food from baskets and fly flat things they called kites high in the air.

It's too bad Beau and Sylvie aren't here, thought Nadine. I'll have to tell them everything that happens. Beau and Sylvie were her best friends. Today they were visiting their aunt on the other side of the hill.

Nadine watched the man help the woman out of the carriage. The children—a boy and a girl—scrambled from behind her and started running up the slope. The boy held a brightly patterned kite in one hand.

"Carolina! Marcel! Be careful. You'll fall," called the woman. She climbed the hill slowly, lifting the hem of her long skirt above the dirt and grass. She carried a picnic basket that looked as if it were made of twigs. Her hat, blue as the sky, was topped with a cloud of white feathers.

The man followed, smiling. He cradled something in his arms. It made Nadine think of an upside-down tortoise with head and legs pulled inside. But as she stared harder, Nadine could see it wasn't a turtle. It was a box, and something like a stick poked out of one end. As the man walked, he started to twist it in a circle.

Nadine couldn't believe her ears: Sounds like bird songs spilled out of the box. No. The sounds were like wind sighs. No. What were they like? There was a pattern to them: high and low; fast and slow. As she listened, Nadine couldn't help moving her head from side to side.

Then she noticed the children were getting close to her special rock. She slipped down to the grass, backing into her favorite shade-hole in the dirt, where she could safely watch.

Marcel released his kite on the faint breeze. It floated skyward, tugging at the end of its long string. Carolina started picking flowers close to Nadine's hiding place. She picked spurge, wild lavender, and thyme. Nadine's mouth watered: Those were her favorite snacks.

"Maman," called Carolina, holding up her small bunch. "See my flowers!"

Maman set the picnic basket down and looked. "Beautiful." She took out a cloth and spread it on the grass, then sat.

"Papa, see how high my kite is," yelled Marcel.

"High indeed," said Papa. He set the strange box down beside the basket; then laid his hat next to the box.

"Children, come and sit." Maman patted the ground. "It's time to eat."

People are so odd, Nadine thought. Not a single leaf in their meal. There never is. To her horror, Carolina tucked her flowers into the cloud of feathers on Maman's hat. A waste of good food! Nadine closed her eyes.

When she opened them again, Maman was breaking what looked like a smooth brown branch into chunks.

Nadine knew from other picnics this was something called a baguette. She knew what was coming next. But it was too late to move without someone seeing her. She shuddered as Maman took out the horrible yellow cheese that made Nadine's nose-holes ache.

"I love cheese," said Carolina with a happy sigh as Maman cut it into pieces to go with the bread.

Ugh! thought Nadine. She was glad when Maman finally wrapped it up and put it back in the basket.

When the family finished their meal, Marcel wanted to fly his kite again.

"It's my turn," complained Carolina.

He jutted his chin at her. "It's my kite."

The corners of Carolina's mouth turned down. "You have to share!"

Papa reached over and smoothed her pale hair. "What do you care about flying a kite?" he asked. He smiled. "You can fly with the music from our music box, eh?" He lifted the strange box with the stick and put it in his lap.

Nadine stretched her neck to see a little better. "Music box," she told herself. "I must remember what they call it. How upset Beau and Sylvie will be to find out what they missed!"

"When he turns the handle, do your pretty dance," Maman told Carolina.

Nadine watched Carolina's father twist the stick in a circle again. Out came the wondrous sounds she'd heard earlier.

Carolina stopped pouting. She stood on tiptoe and began to step to the music. Her thin legs in pale green stockings looked like flower stems that could move. She put a foot out to one side, then to the other. She twirled, and her pink pinafore fluttered like flower petals in a breeze. She lifted her small arms above her head. Nadine thought of delicate tubes in the centers of flowers, where butterflies flew down to drink.

Even Marcel stopped flying his kite to watch.

Papa twisted the stick faster. The music sped up. Carolina twirled three times and took little running steps. He slowed the music, and she swayed from side to side. On and on the music floated on the air, now fast, now slow.

Finally, Carolina paused and put one toe forward, stretching her arms out at either side. Papa stopped turning the handle. The music stopped.

"That was my flower dance," she said.

"Bravo," cried Papa.

"Lovely," said Maman.

They brought their hands together quickly, several times. Each time their hands touched, they made a sharp noise.

Carolina seemed to like the funny sound, for she said, "Thank you."

"Remember to bow," said Maman. Carolina held the hem of her pink pinafore on each side and bent forward from the waist.

Nadine cocked her head. How wonderful, this flower dance and this bowing! With the music still humming in her head, she sighed. "Beau and Sylvie will never believe me."

Carolina's father took what looked like a round, flat stone from his pocket. It gleamed in the sunlight as he squinted at it. "Time to go home," he said.

Nadine blinked. How could he know that from looking at a small, shiny stone?

But the children seemed to understand. They helped Maman pack the basket and fold the cloth.

"I'll carry the basket," said Marcel, as if to make up for his stinginess with the kite. Papa picked up the marvelous box, taking Carolina's hand in his free hand, and the family started down the hill.

Long after the clip-clop of horse hooves faded, Nadine remained in her hole, her chin on the ground. Again, she heard the music and saw Carolina dance her beautiful flower dance. Round and round the music went in her head, like the box's handle. Slow and fast, the tune rose and fell in her heart. How she wished she could dance!

54

An idea began to form. It grew and grew until it, too, went round and round in her head with the music. Maybe I can dance if I try.

Nadine climbed out of her hole, looking this way and that. Suddenly she was glad that Beau and Sylvie had gone to visit their aunt. There was no one to see if she failed.

She lumbered over to her rock. Pressing the claws of her front feet against the side, she pulled herself up until she was upright. She leaned against the rock and looked down, growing dizzy. How far away the grass and flowers seemed!

"I'm not here to look at grass," Nadine told herself. She let go of the rock and tried to take a few steps to the music in her head. She teetered to one side and fell, landing on her back next to a small sapling. Huffing and puffing, she managed to scrabble at the young tree and get right side up.

Tortoises aren't meant to dance, she thought sadly. But inside her heart, the music still played. She pushed herself up on all fours. "No. I'll try again," she said.

Nadine crawled to the rock and used her front feet again to creep up the side until she was standing. Now it felt exciting to be so high in the air. She let go of the rock. This time she took several more steps before falling.

"That wasn't so bad," she told herself. Grunting, she crawled back to the rock. "Carolina's father made the music go faster and slower," she reminded herself. Maybe she could make the music go slower in her head.

She tried that and it worked! She was able to take five steps, turn, and wave her front legs before she fell. "I'll make it go even slower," she decided. All afternoon Nadine practiced, slowing the music more and more, until finally it was just right.

She stepped to one side, then the other. She turned three times. She moved from side to side, pretending her thick legs were the lower branches of a shrub. She swayed her head like a cluster of berries waving in a breeze. She lifted her front legs above her head. Their black and gold markings were like the patterns of sun and leaf shadows on branches. She closed her eyes, stepping, turning, and swaying to the slow, beautiful music in her head.

I should end the dance like Carolina did, she thought, wondering how to bow. She opened her eyes. To her surprise, Beau and Sylvie were stretched out on a dirt mound, watching. Both were moving their heads back and forth, as if they could hear the music, too. Nadine paused and so did they.

"That was wonderful," said Beau. "What do you call it?"

Warmth wafted through Nadine like a ray of sunshine. She held her front legs out at each side and put one back foot forward, the way Carolina had. Afraid a bow like Caroline's would make her fall, Nadine simply lowered her head.

"That was my shrub dance," she said.

Friends for Life

Émile put one of the small riding chairs and its ladder on Angelique,
and Pierre climbed up and sat.

Once upon a Paris zoo, an orphaned elephant entered her new home. Three other elephants watched as the zookeeper led Angelique into the yard. Swallowing her fright, she looked around: From one side, a giraffe peered over his fence. Across from him, a rhinoceros glared through his bars. Behind her, Pierre's voice called, "Goodbye, Angelique."

Angelique looked back at the small, chubby boy she'd grown to love. He blew her a kiss. His father, Monsieur Garnier, looked solemn in the dark frock coat and top hat he wore.

A belly rumble made Angelique turn again. One of the elephants, the elderly one, came toward Angelique, lifting her trunk in greeting.

"Welcome to the Jardin des Plantes," she said. "I am Sophie."

Shyly, Angelique held up her own trunk. The two other elephants stayed at the doorway of the shelter.

"Take good care of Angelique, Émile," Monsieur Garnier told the zookeeper. "She is special."

The keeper's weathered face reddened. "I do my job, Monsieur. I know she saved Pierre's life, but she is an animal, not a queen."

Monsieur Garnier fingered his silky mustache. "For saving Pierre, she is a princess. Remember: I work in the office. I'll be reporting her progress to the managers."

Angelique pulled her rope loose from Émile's hand and ran to the gate. Through the bars, she wrapped her trunk around Pierre's wrist.

Émile walked over and picked up her rope. In a grudging tone, he told Monsieur Garnier, "I haven't forgotten you also saved my life."

Monsieur Garnier patted Angelique's trunk. To his son, he said, "Come, Pierre, I must get to my office, and you must let your friend settle into her new home."

"Remember, we are friends for life," Pierre told Angelique. "I'll visit you every day."

After they left, Émile inspected Angelique's trunk and lifted her large ears, grousing, "An animal is an animal."

Sophie sent comforting belly rumbles to Angelique. "Act cheerful," she advised. She swung her trunk to indicate the two large elephants who still stared in silence. "Be like Castor and Pollux. They romp and play. Visitors like that, and they give treats. Émile gives treats, too."

"Castor and Pollux aren't very friendly," Angelique said in a low voice, as the keeper examined first one foot, then another.

"Pollux," Sophie rumbled with authority. "Come here with your brother and be polite."

Pollux walked over and barely touched her trunk to Angelique's. Sulkily, she muttered, "Pierre's father never checks on us."

"Did you really save Pierre's life?" Castor asked.

Angelique nodded. "There was a train wreck."

But Émile had finished examining Angelique. "No lingering damage from the trip," he said. He led her into the tall shelter. The stench of moldy hay made her gasp.

"So, my fine princess," Émile said. "I'll leave you to your palace and get on with my chores." He untied the rope around her neck.

"Do something friendly," said Sophie, who had followed.

Angelique shyly patted Émile's arm with her trunk.

63

A lopsided smile creased his face. "You're a sweet one." He reached into the pocket of his shabby jacket and gave her a piece of bread.

After he left, Castor hurried in, Pollux behind him. "Tell us about the train wreck," said. Castor.

Memories flooded through Angelique. The train had been the last part of her journey. Before that she had walked across the African desert with people who had killed her mother. Someone bought her and put her on a boat. Someone else bought her and she was on a big ship. The ship arrived at a city her owners called Marseille. They kept her in a large yard for days. Angelique blinked back tears: She had been so alone!

"Where did the wreck happen?" Castor's question interrupted her thoughts.

"The train left Marseille," she said. "That's where I was when Pierre and his father and Émile came to get me. They put me in a special box . . . ."

"A boxcar," said Pollux. She waved her trunk airily. "We've all been on trains."

"Émile rode in the boxcar with me," said Angelique. "Pierre wanted to ride with me, too. He knew I was scared." She fell silent, thinking of how Pierre always understood her. She was glad he was going to visit every day.

"Go on," Castor said.

"His father let him ride with us. I could see light from a small window. We rode all day and part of the night. And then," Angelique frowned, "I don't know exactly what happened. There was a crash. My boxcar bumped hard against something. It went into the air and came down again. I smashed up against the door." She shivered.

Sophie stroked Angelique's head with her trunk. "You poor dear, it must have been terrible!"

"How did you save Pierre?" Castor asked impatiently.

"The door broke open. I fell out. I could smell smoke. Monsieur Garnier was lying on the ground. I realized Pierre was still in the boxcar and it was burning. I rushed back inside.

Angelique saw again Pierre's silent form, lying as if asleep.

"A piece of metal from the door frame had knocked Émile down," she told her listeners. "He couldn't get up, so I grabbed Pierre by the waist and pulled him out. By then, Monsieur Garnier had managed to get to his feet. When he saw Pierre was safe, he went into the boxcar and helped Émile out. Just in time. A moment later the car was on fire."

"You were lucky," Castor said.

Angelique barely heard him. The long months of travel had worn her out. "I'd like to sleep for a while," she said.

Time passed slowly at the Jardin des Plantes. Angelique tried to get used to her new life. Winter brought something white and cold called snow that melted in warm spring rains. Summer breezes blew unfamiliar scents from leafy trees outside the gate.

Pierre came every day after school. His father came twice, once at lunch, and again with his son. But it was Pierre's visits Angelique waited for.

"Don't forget," he would say, as she reached her trunk through the bars to stroke his face. "We are friends for life."

Sophie continued to give advice. "Be lively," she urged. "Trot around and look happy. Children like that. Don't be like Jumbo."

"Jumbo?"

"An elephant who lived here a few years ago. The keepers never liked him. He was too quiet and timid. And when these two came," Sophie nodded toward Castor and Pollux, "they were such show-offs, Jumbo was completely ignored."

"It's not our fault they liked us better," said Pollux.

"They neglected all the animals," Castor added. "Émile was careless about feeding times. He didn't always wash us, either."

"At least you got some attention. Jumbo fell sick and nearly died," Sophie reminded him.

"They traded him to another zoo for that awful rhinoceros next door," Pollux told Angelique.

"Things are better now," Castor said. "There was so much fuss about Jumbo, the keepers had to improve. Even Émile."

"The shelter could still be cleaner," Sophie said.

More months went by. Castor and Pollux were a little friendlier, but mostly they kept to themselves. The giraffe next door paced back and forth. The rhinoceros still glared through his bars. Mice scampered into the yard with gossip: A zebra had dug holes in the dirt with his hooves. A camel was spitting at people.

Angelique tried to take heart from the families who visited the zoo. Children laughed and fed her cakes or bread. But they always wandered off to look at other animals. Sometimes Castor and Pollux were taken somewhere to give children rides. The keepers would put decorated chairs with ladders on them and lead them out the gate. Angelique was always left behind.

"Angelique's growing," Monsieur Garnier said one day. He twisted the end of his silky mustache, looking pleased.

"Six feet tall," Émile boasted. "I feed her well, eh?"

"He feeds us all better than he used to," Sophie muttered. Even so, Angelique noticed how frail the elderly elephant looked.

One morning, Sophie lay motionless beside her pile of hay. Angelique rumbled softly, urging her to rise.

"No," Sophie said softly. "It's my time to go."

"Please don't go," Angelique begged. "You're like a grandmother to me."

But Sophie closed her eyes. Beneath her trunk, her smile looked peaceful. Angelique trumpeted for the zookeeper. When Émile finally came, it was too late.

The three elephants wept. Castor and Pollux comforted each other. Angelique grieved alone, standing in the shelter for hours, swinging her trunk back and forth.

Émile tried to cheer her up whenever he bathed or fed her. "It will pass," he said one morning. "All things pass." He slapped his cheeks with both hands. "What's this? Now I talk to elephants?"

Only Pierre could comfort her. He patted Angelique's ears and trunk, reminding her, "We are friends for life." Slowly her spirits lifted.

68

Again, summer faded into fall. Something bad was happening outside the Jardin des Plantes. Angelique saw it in the visitors' faces. Parents smiled sadly as their children peeked through bars at the animals. Bread and cake treats stopped. Fewer people came.

After a while, just Pierre and his father visited. Monsieur Garnier and Émile talked about something called war. From what Angelique could figure out, war made people kill each other. Distant explosions and the smell of smoke reminded her of the train wreck.

Then snow blanketed the ground again. The two men spoke of an army surrounding Paris. Émile gave the elephants smaller amounts of hay, muttering, "Food is scarce for us all."

"This is like old times," Pollux complained.

But Angelique noticed how bony Émile's wrists looked below his sleeves. Pierre's round face had become thin and pinched. Monsieur Garnier's frock coat hung on him as if too large.

One afternoon Pierre was unusually quiet while he petted Angelique. Castor and Pollux had gone into the shelter to forage through scraps of hay. Finally, Pierre broke his silence. "Don't worry, Angelique. We'll take care of you."

Don't worry about what? Angelique glanced at Monsieur Garnier and Émile, deep in conversation. She lifted her large ears to listen.

"They've sold the camels?" Émile shook his head, a pained look on his face. "I suppose now the restaurants will offer camel stew."

"People are so hungry, they will eat anything," Monsieur Garnier said.

"I myself have been eating rat pie," Émile admitted. His shoulders slumped. "Ah, Monsieur, the camels were hungry, too. Perhaps it is for the best."

Monsieur Garnier pinched the space between his brows, as if he had a headache. "Today the managers told me that Monsieur Deboos made an offer for Castor and Pollux. Tomorrow someone is coming to . . .." He pressed his lips together. "Tomorrow we must take Angelique someplace where she can't see . . .."

"Papa," Pierre interrupted. "Tomorrow Émile and I can teach Angelique how to give rides."

"Good idea," Émile agreed.

Excited, Angelique forgot the strange conversation. At last she could go with Castor and Pollux and give rides, just as they did!

Early next morning, Émile put one of the small riding chairs and its ladder on Angelique, and Pierre climbed up and sat. For some reason, Castor and Pollux weren't going. Angelique felt so important, she almost forgot she hated being in the zoo. As Émile led her out the gate, she made her steps slow and careful, mindful of Pierre on her back.

The zookeeper led them down a wide path edged by tall leafless trees with patchy trunks. He took them to a far corner of the Jardin des Plantes. Paths wound through bare trees and webby bushes. Leaf litter crunched under Angelique's feet. Despite the cold, her heart was light. How free it felt to be outside the fenced yard!

All morning they roamed the paths, Pierre the only rider. After a lunch of stale bread, they continued their walks until early evening.

"A good training session," Émile said, on the way back to the elephant area.

That's why Castor and Pollux didn't come, Angelique thought. They're already trained.

Monsieur Garnier was at the gate when they returned. "It's over," he said.

Émile led Angelique into the yard. Pierre climbed down. As the keeper removed the chair and its ladder, Angelique looked around for Castor and Pollux, eager to tell them of her day. Where were they? Suddenly uneasy, she ran to the door of the shelter. They weren't inside. She trumpeted for them, but there was no answer. There was a strange smell that frightened her.

"So," Émile said to Pierre's father in a broken voice, "now the restaurants can serve elephant steaks." He brushed away tears with a sleeve.

Numbness spread through Angelique as yesterday's conversation came back to her: Camel stew. Rat pie. Now elephants were being eaten.

"We are going to save you," Pierre told her.

"Come at midnight," Émile advised Monsieur Garnier, "when the city sleeps. Otherwise, people might attack her for food."

Clouds covered the moon when they came. Angelique heard the key clink as Émile unlocked the gate. Soon Pierre and his father and the zookeeper were beside her. Émile tied a long rope around her neck. "Goodbye, Angelique," he whispered.

Monsieur Garnier and Pierre led her through the gate, out of the Jardin des Plantes, and down the lane to their horse-drawn carriage.

"You must run behind us," Pierre explained, while his father tied her rope to the back of the carriage. Then Monsieur Garnier climbed up and sat behind the two horses. Pierre joined them.

Except for the muffled sound of the horses' wrapped hooves, the night was hushed. Angelique loped behind the carriage, dirt and snow crunching beneath her feet. Memories returned of running free across African plains.

They went south along the Seine River, away from the city. The moon came from behind the clouds, splashing light on dark rooftops. The starless night faded to dull gray. As sunrise turned undersides of clouds pink, they came to the edge of a forest.

"Go deep into the Fontainebleau Forest and stay there," Monsieur Garnier told her. She lowered her head.

Pierre burst into tears and pressed his face against her neck. "Don't forget me," he said. "I'll never forget you."

"Hurry," whispered his father.

Angelique gave a low rumble. If only they understood elephant talk! She started running, her heart heavy with all she wanted to say.

"I'll never forget you," she would tell Pierre. "We are friends for life."

The Mighty Leap

Jo-Jo peeped out of Mother's pouch, his little head all ears and eyes.

Once upon a mulga woods, a kangaroo named Minkie propped herself on one elbow, sulking. Her mob napped around her in the shade. Her sister Jilli sprawled beside her, like a small lump of clay against the red Australian dirt. The shaded border at the edge of the mulga woods, the mob's favorite napping place, looked out onto a dry plain.

Everyone else was asleep, but Minkie was restless. Now that Mother was busy with little Jo-Jo, it was Minkie's job to watch Jilli.

No one ever thinks about me, Minkie thought. It isn't fair! She sat up, balancing with her tail, and stared across the red dirt.

Beyond the dirt plain was a meadow. Beyond the meadow, a eucalyptus forest hulked in mystery. Stories were told of the Wise One, an ancient roo who lived inside the forest and was said to have powers. The Wise One drank only rain water, it was said. She ate magic from the air.

A distant rumbling interrupted Minkie's thoughts. It sounded like one of the horse-drawn wagons of the Fire-stick people who shot fire from long sticks and killed kangaroos. She jumped up, thumping the ground with her back foot. Mother and Father raised their heads.

"What is it?" Mother called. Jo-Jo peeped out of her pouch, his little head all ears and eyes.

"Fire-stick people," said Minkie.

Father leaped to his feet, swiveling his red ears. He thumped the ground loudly. "Fire-stick people!" he shouted.

Kangaroos sprang up all around, calling to one another.

"Where's Jilli?" cried Mother.

Minkie stared at the empty spot where Jilli had been. "She was over there!"

"Here I am." Jilli peered from behind a shaggy bush.

Mother frowned at Minkie. "How many times do I have to tell you to stay with Jilli?"

"It's not my fault she hid," protested Minkie. "It's not fair to get mad at me!"

"Don't argue with your mother," Father said. To the mob, he yelled, "Head for the woods."

Jo-Jo clutched Mother's pouch. Minkie grabbed Jilli. They scattered with the rest of the mob, thudding through the taller mulga trees. Overhead, the gray leaves shook on their scraggly branches.

As she hopped, Minkie peeked over her shoulder. Through the trees, she saw the Fire-stick man on his horse-drawn wagon, rumbling across the plain. Dust puffs kicked up from the horse's hooves. In the distance, a flock of pink galah birds rose above the eucalyptus trees.

"Minkie, pay attention," warned Father, suddenly at her side.

"Minkie, hurry up!" called Mother, ahead of them.

Minkie turned and speeded up.

"Minkie, don't yank me so fast!" complained Jilli.

Minkie do this; don't do that, Minkie thought angrily, as they went deep into the woods to safety. No one even thanked me for warning them about the Fire-stick man. No one appreciates anything I do.

In a small clearing inside the woods, Minkie spied her friend Bakana. Bakana's younger sister, Yani, bounded over to Jilli. Bakana and Minkie clicked their hellos as their parents talked.

"Minkie, we'll go check on the rest of the mob," Mother said. "Watch Jilli until we get back. Stay here in the clearing, where it's safe." She and Father bounded away with Bakana's parents. Jo-Jo grinned and waved from Mother's pouch.

"All I do is watch Jilli," Minkie muttered to Bakana. She kicked a spray of dirt in the air.

Jilli and Yani hopped up to her.

"Minkie, tell us a story," said Jilli. "Tell us again how First Kangaroo learned to leap."

"I'm sick of that story," Minkie groused.

Bakana gave her a puzzled frown. "Why are you so cross with them today?"

Minkie glared. "Mother scolds me. Father scolds me. Now you're scolding me."

"A story will keep them occupied," Bakana pointed out.

Minkie sighed. "Oh, all right." She sat back on her haunches.

"Long ago," she began, "First Kangaroo was chased by a Spear-man. Spear-people were here before Fire-stick people came," she reminded her listeners. "They were here since dreamtime—like the Wise One." Minkie paused. Maybe she should talk to The Wise One.

"Go on," Jilli urged, snuggling down beside Yani.

"First Kangaroo couldn't run fast on all fours." Minkie continued. "The man came closer . . ." On and on, the story went, with First Kangaroo learning he could run faster on his back feet like the man.

"Then he took a mighty leap . . ." Minkie stopped again. A mighty leap! "Then he took another," she said. "Soon First Kangaroo discovered he could go faster and farther that way. And that's the reason we hop the way we do today."

Jilli and Yani had both gone to sleep.

"It's been a big day for them," Bakana said.

Minkie nodded, but a plan had formed in her mind. "Bakana," she whispered, "I'm going to leave home."

Bakana gasped. "Why?"

"Everyone scolds me. No one cares how I feel. No one appreciates anything I do."

"Who will watch Jilli?" interrupted Bakana.

Minkie scowled and put her front paws on her hips. "That's just it! Wait and see: When Jo-Jo's out of the pouch, I'll have to watch him too. Mother already said another joey is on the way."

Bakana opened her mouth, then closed it. "Where will you go?" she finally asked. "If you go off alone, a dingo could catch you." Minkie shivered, thinking of the wild dogs that hunted kangaroos. For a moment, she wondered if she should go. But something had to change.

"I'll ask the Wise One for advice," she said. "Maybe she can give me a mighty leap. Then I can go far away, and nothing can catch me."

"The Wise One!" Bakana shuddered. "Is that a good idea? No one really knows what she's like."

"She's called the Wise One for a reason," Minkie said. "Will you help me?"

"Yes," said Bakana, but her forehead drew up in wrinkles of worry.

Just then Minkie's parents came bounding through the trees.

"Everything's safe," said Father. "No sign of any other Fire-people."

"We can go back to our naps," said Mother. "Bakana, your parents are spreading the word. You and Yani come along with us."

"Tonight, I'll bring Jilli to the clearing," Minkie whispered to her friend, as they hopped to the edge of the woods. "If you'll watch her with Yani, I can go see the Wise One." Bakana nodded, but she still looked upset.

That evening, when the mob was in one part of the grassy meadow, foraging for food, Minkie asked Mother if she could forage with Bakana.

"We want to go to the clearing inside the woods," she said.

"Take Jilli with you," said Mother. "And stay together."

Minkie scowled. "I know. I know. Come on," she grumped at Jilli. They hopped to the clearing and found their friends nibbling at clumps of grass.

Minkie gnawed on some roots to calm the quivering in her stomach. Then she whispered to Bakana, "I think I'm ready."

Bakana's eyes widened. "What if a fox gets you?"

Minkie gulped, then shook off her fear. She looked over at the two younger sisters who were giggling together. "Keep Jilli busy, so she won't tell Mother. Tell her we're playing a game and that I'm hiding."

Bakana grimaced. "All right. But hurry. I'll worry until you come back."

Minkie felt a surge of gratitude. For a moment, she wished she wasn't running away. "But," she told herself, "I have to do what I have to do."

Her heart fluttering, Minkie hopped through the trees and across the dirt to the meadow, where she crouched down to avoid being seen. Then she set off for the eucalyptus forest, the tall meadow grasses hiding her from the rest of the mob.

As she entered the forest, the air turned chilly. Minkie thudded through brush and around tall trees, trying not to be frightened. From somewhere, a dingo moaned. She shivered. An owl flew overhead with a great flapping of its wings. Minkie gulped. In the distance, a fox barked.

Finally, she came to a patch of grass lit by the rising moon. There was the Wise One, sitting on her haunches, balancing on her tail. The ancient roo's long face was streaked with gray. Her forehead was heavily furrowed. Her tapering ears stood straight up.

The Wise One narrowed her eyes, studying Minkie. "Why have you come?"

A prickly feeling ran down Minkie's spine. To show respect, she lowered herself to the ground, her head quivering. "Wise One, I wish to leave home." She took a quick peek over her paws.

In the moonlight, the ancient roo's eyes, large and bright, held Minkie in their gaze.

"Why do you wish such a thing?"

"Everyone scolds me and tells me what to do. It's 'Minkie this', or 'Minkie that'. No one cares what I want. Nobody thanks me when I do something." Minkie's voice shook, and she blinked back tears.

"Serious problems," said the Wise One. "But what is your main complaint?"

Minkie hung her head. In a low voice, she said, "No one appreciates me."

"Ah." The Wise One nodded. "Quite serious. And where do you want to go?"

"I'm not sure," said Minkie. "I thought you could advise me."

"Hmm." The Wise One scratched one ear. "What do you hope to find?"

Minkie thought. "I want to go where I'm appreciated," she finally mumbled.

"You are not afraid of dangers?"

Minkie looked up. Eagerly she said, "If you could give me a mighty leap, I'm sure I could escape them."

The ancient roo closed her eyes and kept them closed for a long time. Just when Minkie wondered if she had fallen asleep, the Wise One opened her eyes, and scratched her ear again. "A mighty leap. Mighty enough to escape danger, and to take you to where you are appreciated. I can do that for you."

"Really?" Minkie gave a pleased hop.

"But you must do three things for me."

Minkie nodded.

"First, bring me some water to drink."

Minkie blinked. "But it is said you only drink rain water."

The Wise One waved a front paw. "Stories. Bring me some water."

Minkie hopped and searched until she found a water hole. She filled her pouch and returned, emptying the water into the hollow of a large flat rock.

"That was good," said the Wise One, when she finished lapping the water. "Now bring me some bluebells to eat."

"But it is said you eat magic from the air."

"Bluebells are a special treat," the Wise One said.

In the moonlit night, Minkie hopped back to the grassy field and gathered the blue flowers, returning with a full pouch.

The Wise One happily chewed the flowers, smacked her lips, and wiped her muzzle with both paws. "Now," she said. "Bring me a white stone that is round and flat and smooth."

The moon was high as Minkie hopped back to Bakana in the clearing. Their two sisters were peeking under scrubby bushes and around the mulga trees.

"There she is!" cried Jilli. "I saw her first. I win!" She bounded to Minkie, hugging her. "I don't like this game! Stay here and chase me instead." She bounded to Yani again.

Bakana sidled up to Minkie. "What took you so long?" she whispered. "I was running out of places for them to look."

"I had to fetch water and bluebells," Minkie whispered back. "And now she wants a special stone."

"What's she like?"

"Very old. Kind of bossy. But only a little bit scary."

Jilli hopped back with Yani beside her. "Why is everybody whispering?"

"We're thinking of a new game," Minkie said. "Let's find a pretty stone that looks like the moon."

They searched through the tall grasses and scraped in the dry dirt, finding many pebbles. Some were flat, but rough; some smooth, but lumpy; some round, but not flat. Finally, they found a stone that was just right.

"Wait here," Minkie said. "I have to give this to someone."

When Minkie gave the stone to the Wise One, the ancient roo placed it between her paws and rubbed it. "Describe again what you wish to find."

Minkie folded her arms and frowned, thinking of how everyone ordered her or scolded her and no one thanked her. "A place where I'm appreciated!"

The Wise One smiled a private smile. She set the stone on the ground and tapped it three times before looking up. "There," she said, as if the magic were already in place.

Minkie crouched low, quivering her head to show thanks.

"It's time to go," said the Wise One.

"I'll go say my goodbyes," said Minkie. But an ache started to spread through her chest.

"No," said the Wise One. "It is time to go now, to your new land."

Minkie blinked. "Right now?"

"Close your eyes, make your wish, and leap," said the ancient roo. "Keep in mind what you hope to find. At sunrise, you will be where you are appreciated."

"But," said Minkie.

The Wise One reared back on her haunches, folding her front arms. She seemed to swell in size. "We have spent the night preparing for this," she said.

"Yes," whispered Minkie.

"Make your wish and leap."

"Maybe—" began Minkie.

"Leap," the Wise One commanded.

Her heart heavy, Minkie thumped her tail against the ground and shot into the air. Up, up, up, she soared into the night sky. The moon lay against the darkness like a round white stone. Stars glowed above, like Spear-people's campfires. Higher and higher Minkie sailed, trying to concentrate on her new life where no one would scold her and everyone would appreciate her.

Instead, the memory of Jilli's hug came to mind, followed by Jo-Jo's grinning face as he waved from Mother's pouch. She saw Mother's tired face after a night of foraging. She thought of Bakana's loyalty, and the way Father watched out for everyone's safety.

"When have I thanked them?" Minkie asked herself. "Oh, why did leaving seem like such a good idea? Now who will help Mother with Jo-Jo when he's too big for the pouch? Who will tell Jilli stories? Bakana and I could forage and joey-sit together. Why didn't I think of that before?"

As love and concern seeped through Minkie's heart, the moon and stars began to fade. The darkness around her lightened to gray. Before she knew it, she was floating down again. Soon she drifted through pink-stained clouds over the mulga woods and landed in the little clearing where she had left Jilli and Bakana and Yani earlier.

Jilli hopped over and hugged her again.

"Did you give the Wise One the stone?" asked Bakana. She looked close to tears. "When do you leave?"

"I already did," whispered Minkie. "But, I missed everyone and came back."

"Really!" A smile spread across Bakana's face.

Minkie took her paw. "I'll tell you all about it," she said. "Right now, let's go join the others."

The roos were all settling after their night of foraging. Seeing her family, Minkie wanted to turn somersaults. She was home again, where she belonged.

Most Beautiful of All

"Away to Nerina and her foolish claim!"

O nce upon the Aegean Sea in ancient Greece, three sea nymphs played water tag. A fourth sat on a rocky reef close to shore. The sea nymphs were water goddesses who looked like beautiful young women. They lived in a silvery cave at the bottom of the sea, but they liked to frolic in the ocean waves. All except Nerina.

Nerina gazed with love at her image in a shell she had polished to a high sheen. I'm the most beautiful goddess of all, she thought.

Growing tired of their game, the other three swam to the reef and climbed up beside Nerina to sun themselves. She tore her gaze from her reflection.

"Am I not beautiful?" she said. It wasn't the first time. Her companions frowned and were silent.

"My beautiful hair is as deep a blue as the sea," Nerina continued, combing her fingers through her ringlets. "My eyes as turquoise as the sky."

"Nerina," said one of the other sea goddesses. "We all have blue hair and turquoise eyes."

Nerina turned to look at her. "Not as beautiful as mine."

A second goddess scowled. "You think too much of yourself."

Nerina pouted. "Good friends shouldn't criticize."

"Good friends tell the truth," said the third goddess. "You shouldn't boast."

Nerina tossed her head and returned to gazing at her image. "I'm the most beautiful of all," she insisted. "Probably more beautiful than Aphrodite."

"More beautiful than Aphrodite?" her companions chorused. Aphrodite was the Goddess of Beauty. She was one of the twelve Olympian gods and goddesses. And the Olympians ruled over all other gods and goddesses on land or sea, including nymphs.

"Be careful," warned the first sea nymph. "You know Aphrodite was declared the most beautiful goddess of all in a contest."

"You know how vain she is," added the second.

"And she has spies everywhere," said the third, looking around nervously.

Indeed, two seahorses had been listening at the side of the reef. They nodded their spiny horse heads at each other. Aphrodite, they remembered, was visiting her Uncle Poseidon, the God of the Sea, in his coral palace on the ocean floor. Winding their curled tails even tighter, the two spies swam straight to Aphrodite and reported Nerina's boast.

"More beautiful than me? The Goddess of Beauty?" Aphrodite gave a scornful laugh, sending bubbles through the salty water.

"That's what she claims," said one seahorse.

"You shall catch many shrimp for telling me this," Aphrodite promised. "Who is this foolish creature? Where can I find her?"

They told her.

Aphrodite smoothed her shimmering toga, which was woven from sea foam and stardust. Winding a long golden tendril of hair around her finger, she turned to Poseidon.

"Uncle," she said, "I know the sea is your realm, but may I have power over this one little sea nymph?" When he hesitated, she added, "You wouldn't want some unimportant sea god claiming to be more powerful than you are."

"Of course not!" said Poseidon. "Such things can't be allowed." He pounded his trident on the ocean floor, causing a tidal wave to swallow up an island above them.

"Do I have your permission to teach her a lesson?" asked Aphrodite.

"Indeed," said Poseidon, straightening his gold crown and smoothing his long silvery beard. "It's a matter of honor."

Aphrodite set about her plan. First, she made herself tiny. Then she harnessed the seahorses to a small open clam shell. Raising a hand, she chanted,

"Away to Nerina and her foolish claim.

Away to this upstart who'd outdo my fame."

When Aphrodite arrived, Nerina was still looking at herself in her seashell mirror. The other nymphs were sunning themselves on the reef. Glancing down, one of them spied the clamshell coach with its tiny passenger.

"How beautiful," she exclaimed.

Nerina peered to see. "What a charming little thing," she agreed. She reached down and untied the seahorses, lifting the clamshell onto her palm. Smiling at tiny Aphrodite, she said, "You are almost as beautiful as I am!"

Scarcely were the words out of Nerina's mouth when Aphrodite let herself grow to her giant height. Nerina froze with fear. The other nymphs leaped into the water, swimming away in a froth of splashes.

"Repeat what you said," Aphrodite ordered.

Nerina opened her mouth, but not a sound came out.

"Almost as beautiful?" Aphrodite reminded her.

"Please forgive me," begged Nerina.

Aphrodite gazed on the trembling sea nymph. Knowing that some apologies come from true remorse and others from only fear, she said, "Perhaps you can redeem yourself."

"Oh, yes! Please let me," begged Nerina.

Aphrodite knew that wishes could reveal Nerina's true feelings better than any promises. "I will give you three wishes," she said.

Nerina stopped trembling. "You'll grant me . . . wishes?"

"Indeed, I will," Aphrodite replied. She shrank herself to Nerina's size and sat beside her. "What do you wish for?"

A sly look came over Nerina's face. She tapped her chin and frowned in thought. "I'd like to have friends who would admire me, instead of criticizing me," she said.

Aphrodite narrowed her eyes. Clearly remorse was far from the nymph's heart. "What is your second wish?"

Nerina folded her arms, looking more at ease. "I would like to travel to another land, to even another time, far in the future."

Aphrodite smiled grimly, seeing that Nerina imagined time and distance would put her beyond Aphrodite's reach. "What else?" she asked softly.

"I'd like to be famous for my beauty," Nerina confessed, quickly adding, "Not as famous as you, of course."

Aphrodite placed her hands on Nerina's shoulders and looked into her turquoise eyes. "Your wishes will be granted," she said. "You will be admired by friends. You will travel to another land in a future time. And you will be famous for your beauty." She smiled. "But not the way you think."

"That's so generous," Nerina protested, trying to sound humble. Inside, she gloated: How envious her companions would be!

Aphrodite returned to her giant size and raised a hand. She snapped her fingers with a sound like a rumbling tidal wave.

An icy numbness came over Nerina. Her body began to twist and pull. Her last thought was that her feet must be melting into each other. Looking down, Nerina saw she now had a long, graceful tail in all hues of the rainbow. Then she was whirling through time and space, and her mind went blank.

When Nerina came to, she was surrounded by small, speckled fish she had never seen before. She opened her mouth in surprise and swallowed water. It wasn't salty like the droplets that splashed on her lips when spray hit the rocks at the reef. And she seemed to be breathing the water through her neck! Anxiously Nerina started to lift a hand to her neck, but she couldn't move her arm. She couldn't even see her arms.

She could move her head from side to side, and she glanced around. She was in something like a cave. Was it her silvery home at the bottom of the sea? Nerina swam closer and saw the wall was gray rock. Light filtered down from above through the rippling water. Ahead of her, tunnels branched off, this way and that. More fish swam up to Nerina.

"You're new here, aren't you," one gurgled.

"You're so beautiful," said another.

"Can I be your friend?" several chorused.

Wildly Nerina looked around, hoping to find her reef, where she could sit and think. But there was nothing.

Propelled by her tail, she swam upward, breaking through the water's surface.

Two men stared at her from what looked like a rocky bank. They were dressed differently from Greeks Nerina had seen. Instead of pale togas falling straight from their shoulders, their clothes were black and fitted. Their foot coverings and head coverings were black, too.

The taller man had a thick mustache. He tugged on it now, frowning thoughtfully. They spoke in a language Nerina had never heard, but their words slowly became clear.

"Never have I seen such a beautiful fish, Monsieur Carbonnier," the shorter man said. "And so large, eh? As big as a large cat, wouldn't you say? Or maybe a small dog?"

Monsieur Carbonnier nodded. "The most beautiful fish I have ever seen. Such a long, elegant tail! Such brilliant rainbow colors! And look at its gills—they shine, like gold."

"See how it studies us," said the shorter man in a tone of wonder. "I have never seen turquoise eyes on a fish before, have you?"

The openings in Nerina's neck pumped hard as thoughts raced through her. "Fish? I'm a fish?" She thrashed her tail in terror. Gasping for oxygen, she dived down again.

One of the other fish swam close to Nerina. "You'll get used to life in the aquarium," she said. "My name is Clarabelle," she added. "What is yours?"

Nerina forced herself to breathe slowly, trying to calm herself. "Please," she asked. "Where am I?"

"Why, in the Trocadéro Aquarium, under the Palais du Trocadéro," said Clarabelle. "It's for the Exposition," she explained. "They've built it to look like a river, to make us feel more at home. But, of course, we all know better."

Frightened, Nerina asked, "What's an aquarium?"

Clarabelle blinked in surprise. After a moment, she said gently, "It's a place where humans put fish, so they can study us."

Nerina swam back to the water's surface, not wanting to hear any more. But Clarabelle followed.

"There it is again," said Monsieur Carbonnier. "If only we knew where it came from, or what to call it." He pursed his lips under his thick mustache, then smiled. "Fortunate for us, eh? The whole world is here in Paris for the Exposition, and no other aquarium has such a fish."

His companion nodded. "Even when the Exposition is over, people will come to see it."

Clarabelle nudged Nerina with a fin. "You'll be famous," she said.

"Famous," Nerina whispered. She dove down and swam along the aquarium floor, longing for her silvery cave at the bottom of the sea in ancient Greece.

"Oh, look! It's her!" The earlier school of fish surrounded her, burbling their praise:

"Isn't she adorable?"

"Oh, if only I could be like her!"

"Oh, please, let me be your friend!"

Nerina stared around, remembering her three wishes. Here were friends who admired her. She lived in a land and time far in the future. And she was going to be famous for her beauty.

If a fish could cry, the Trocadéro Aquarium would have overflowed with Nerina's sad tears.

The Burro from La Mancha

An old man in a red cloak stood in their path. His wrinkled face
scowled from under a lumpy red hat.

O nce upon a plain in Spain, a burro named Tulio pulled a plow in a wheat field. He paused to watch a butterfly flit from weed to weed.

Like a flying flower, he thought. How beautiful. How free.

"Worthless beast," cried his owner, Severo. "I can't plow if you stand there dreaming! Wheat can't be planted if the soil isn't tilled!" He whipped Tulio's rump.

Tulio gave a muffled bray in protest. How he envied the butterfly its freedom. Sadly, he trudged back and forth, until the field was furrowed with rows of freshly turned soil. The sun was setting as they returned to the stone farmhouse where Tulio slept in a stall under the living quarters.

A traveling poet came to Severo's gate. "I'll recite a poem for a meal and a place to lay my head," he told the farmer.

"You'll have to recite more than a poem for that," grumbled Severo. Behind him, his children chased each other in the small courtyard, squealing and yelling.

"Do you know any stories?" Severo asked the poet. "If you can keep my children quiet until dinner, I'll give you a meal and let you sleep in the bodega with my burro."

From his stall in the bodega, Tulio pricked up his long ears.

Severo's wife was roasting a lamb over a pit by the courtyard wall. During spring and summer the family ate in the courtyard at a rough wooden table with benches.

"Perhaps you would like to hear the story of Don Quixote," said the poet. "Don Quixote de la Mancha was a knight from this very region."

"Truly?" asked Severo. He sent his oldest son to fetch a stool for the poet, placing it at one end of the table near the bodega. "Stop your quarreling!" he shouted to the children. "Come and listen."

Tulio sidled to the bodega doorway so that he could listen, too.

"There was once a man who read too many books," began the poet. He told how Don Quixote decided to copy

106

the knights in those books, seeking brave adventures and noble deeds.

Tulio and the family listened spellbound from the beginning, when Don Quixote left home to right all wrongs and win the heart of Dulcinea.

After the poet finished his tale, Severo shook his head. "Don Quixote was a foolish dreamer. He should have stayed home."

"Then there would be no story," said the poet.

"A good story it was," Severo admitted. "You have earned your keep."

In the bodega that night, as the poet snored on a pile of straw, Tulio went over the story in his head. I, too, am a dreamer, he thought. Why should I pull a plow and be whipped for admiring a butterfly? I, too, will seek brave adventures and noble deeds.

The next day, after the poet left, Severo planted the wheat. When the sun was overhead, he returned to the farmhouse for lunch. He left Tulio with his flock of sheep in a grassy plot near the woods edging his land.

Tulio watched Severo walk away. El Señor Severo can pull his own plow, he thought. He trotted into the woods to begin his new life.

Soon Tulio was in unfamiliar countryside, passing barley fields and stands of scrubby oaks. All afternoon he traveled dusty roads past trickling streams and picked his way through wheat fields and vineyards. At times, he galloped. Often, he trotted. Sometimes he paused to nibble grass and admire yellow sprays of early broom.

When night fell, he stopped to rest in a forest. Hearing distant grunts of wild boars and the spooky call of an owl, Tulio twitched his ears. Already my life is exciting, he thought.

At sunrise, a desperate braying woke Tulio. He followed the sound to a small olive orchard, where he saw another burro tied to an olive tree. She pawed the bare ground at her feet, crying.

"Dry your tears, for I am here," Tulio said.

The other burro gave him a frightened glance. "Who are you?"

"Don Tulio de la Mancha at your service. Here to right all wrongs."

"El Señor Soto has forgotten me again," she said. "Three days ago, he left me here to graze." New tears rolled from the frightened burro's large dark eyes. "El Soto is old and forgetful. Often, I have spent two days waiting for him to fetch me. But never three. I don't think he's coming back this time. I ate the last of the grass at my feet yesterday."

"Fear not," Tulio said. Immediately he set to work chewing the rope that tied her, until it pulled apart and she was free.

Gratefully she swiveled her ears forward. "How can I thank you?"

"Noble deeds need no thanks. May I know your name?"

"Dulce," she replied. "El Señor Soto says I have a sweet nature." She lowered her eyes.

Tulio's heart thumped as he asked, "Perhaps Dulce is also short for . . . Dulcinea?"

"I know not that name."

"Perhaps you would like to hear the story of Don Quixote."

As Dulce chewed some nearby grass, Tulio recounted the poet's tale of the knight's efforts to win Dulcinea's admiration. He also told of his own life with Severo.

"You were right to leave that cruel farmer," Dulce said.

"And now," said Tulio, his chest swelling, "I will have adventures in your name and return for your admiration."

"Tulio," said Dulce. "I'm not going to let El Soto tie me to a tree and forget me again. I'll have my own adventures. I'm going to Provence."

"Provence?"

"A region in France."

"That's not how the story goes," Tulio objected. "Besides, nobody knows you in France."

"My cousin Felicia lives there," said Dulce. "A few years ago, a visiting farmer from Provence bought her as a present for his son. Felicia says her life is wonderful. Often she has asked me to join her."

Tulio snorted. "How can she speak to you from France?"

"She sends word through an owl, who tells a raven, who tells another raven, who tells a boar, who tells another boar, who tells the owl who lives in Soto's barn. Then I send my answer through that owl, who . . .."

Tulio nodded. "Si, I understand." He wrinkled his brow. If Dulce had adventures of her own, how could he be her hero?

"The farmer and his wife have two more children," Dulce continued. "I'm sure they'd like two more burros. Why don't you come with me?"

"You are changing the story!"

Dulce blinked. "Tulio, this isn't a story. And you'd better leave Spain," she pointed out. "El Señor Severo will be looking for you."

"True," said Tulio. A new thought brightened his heart: If they had adventures on the trip, she'd see his noble deeds right away.

First, they went to the barn, and Dulce sent her message through the owl. Then they set off across the orchard until they came to a winding dirt road. A gushing brook lined with beech trees and oaks ran alongside it.

"You seem to know where you are going," Tulio said.

"Felicia sent directions often. We go north, then east, and then across some mountains."

For the next hour, they quietly followed the road. It narrowed and climbed; then an even narrower path zigzagged through higher woods.

Finally, Dulce paused and said, "Let's rest a bit."

Tulio was happy to agree.

"Tulio," Dulce said. "I don't know why you admire Don Quixote. He was always in trouble. He thought everything was enchanted when it wasn't."

"That is where Don Quixote and I differ," Tulio said. "Like him, I am a dreamer. But I do not believe in enchantments. For," He gave a braying laugh, tossing his head toward a curiously twisted tree at one side of the path, "if I believed in enchantments, I would fool myself that yonder tree is a woman in a brown bark gown with long sleeves. I would imagine those orange leaves are her hair,

111

and she is clutching it in despair. I would think those knot holes were sorrowful eyes, and the bumps below them a delicate nose and pointed chin. But," Tulio assured Dulce, "I know it is only a tree."

"Tulio," whispered Dulce, trembling. "That is a woman. A strange-looking *tree* woman."

Tulio looked again and gulped.

They drew closer, and the woman moaned, "Oh, sorrowful day! Oh, who can help me?"

Tulio galloped to her side. "Don Tulio de la Mancha at your service," he said. "Here to right all wrongs. Who are you?"

"I am Luz, an aloge," she replied.

A water woman! Tulio and Dulce looked at each other.

"An evil brujo named Casimiro put a spell on me," Luz continued, "because I wouldn't obey him and stop curing people in my village."

"Why would a wizard do that?" asked Dulce.

"Casimiro loves sickness and death," said Luz. "Only a brave deed can free me."

"Fear not," said Tulio. "I am here."

"Once I am free," said Luz, "I will grant you one wish."

Tulio's thoughts drifted a moment to Don Quixote. "Perhaps 'Luz' is short for . . . Lucinda?" he said.

"I know not that name."

"Perhaps you would like to hear the story of Don Quixote." Again, Tulio told the tale, including Don Quixote's wish for Dulcinea's admiration and Lucinda's reunion with her true love.

Luz wagged a twiggy finger at Tulio. "Don Quixote was foolish to let people play tricks on him. But I am not looking for my true love. I must return to my village well or die."

Tulio's brow furrowed. A water woman enchanted by a wizard! Life is nothing like that story, he thought.

"Beyond these woods is a village," Luz said. "Below the roots of a giant oak lies the entrance to an underground cave. A duende there guards a glass statue of Casimiro. You must outsmart this duende and smash the statue."

Tulio laid his ears back against his mane and lowered his tail. Carefully he asked, "A duende?" Duendes, he had heard, were ugly little gnomes known for their dangerous cunning.

"The statue he guards holds Casimiro's magic," said Luz. "If you destroy the statue, both Casimiro and the duende will be powerless. Then I can return to my well and cure villagers again."

113

"Tulio can do this," said Dulce.

Tulio lifted his ears and straightened his back, unwilling to disappoint her. "I will return victorious," he promised.

"Keep your eyes fixed on the duende and his eyes on you," Luz advised. "While he's in your stare, he's helpless. Whatever you do, don't blink."

"I'm coming with you," Dulce said. She set off through the woods with Tulio despite his protests.

"I will meet you at the village well," Luz called after them.

When they came to the huge tree, Tulio found the opening at the base of its gnarled trunk behind a thorny bush. He pawed at a tree root. The opening widened to a tunnel. He and Dulce entered, single file, Tulio in front. They followed the sloping floor and came out into a huge room of gleaming rock walls. Stone pillars from ceiling to floor reminded Tulio of drippings from one of El Severo's candles.

An ugly little duende stood in the center of the room, hands on hips. He showed Tulio a smile full of sharp, yellow teeth. "Who are you?" he snarled. "What foolish errand brings you here?"

"Don Tulio de la Mancha," replied Tulio. "I am here to right all wrongs." At the far end of the cave, on a glowing stone, he spied the red glass statue of a man with horns.

"I am Cardo de la Caverna," snarled the duende. "Named 'Cardo' because I eat thistles—unless a tasty burro comes my way!" His harsh laugh racketed off the walls.

"Keep him talking," whispered Dulce.

"You are well-named," Tulio told Cardo. The duende narrowed his eyes at him, and Tulio locked glances with him.

"Perhaps Cardo is also short for . . . Cardenio?" Tulio asked. From the corner of his eye, Tulio saw Dulce edge to the right of a pillar and then behind it.

"I know not that name," said the duende, scowling as he realized he was captured by Tulio's gaze.

"Perhaps you would like to hear the story of Don Quixote."

While Dulce edged along the wall toward the statue, Tulio told Cardo the entire tale. He told of Don Quixote's love of Dulcinea, Cardenio's love for Lucinda, Dorothea's love for Don Fernando, and Sancho Panza's loyalty to poor, confused Don Quixote.

Tulio finished his tale just as Dulce reached the red glass statue.

"Never was a squire more faithful to his master," he added, "than Sancho Panza to Don Quixote."

"That may be," growled Cardo, still struggling against Tulio's steady stare, "but I, too, am faithful, and I serve a master far less foolish than Don Quixote." The duende bared his teeth. "Sooner or later, you will blink."

At that moment, Dulce kicked the red statue high into the air against the rock ceiling of the cave. The glass figure shattered. Its tinkling pieces rained down in a thousand splintered fragments. A howl went up from Cardo. In a glittering poof, he vanished.

Braying with delight, the burros trotted out of the cave. They came around the thorn bush, halting in surprise. An old man in a red cloak stood in their path. His wrinkled face scowled from under a lumpy red hat. Silently he turned and started walking—with a limp, Tulio noticed—down the road leading away from the village.

"That's Casimiro without his power," Tulio whispered. "That means Luz isn't a tree anymore. She's a water woman again."

"The spell is broken," agreed Dulce. "You were so brave."

"We both were brave," Tulio replied.

Luz was at the well, as promised. She held a hazel wand in one hand. Her orange hair fell in burnished waves

116

to her knees. Her silvery-blue dress rippled with highlights like water in a stream. "Well done, noble burros," she said. "What is your wish?"

More noble deeds could make me a real hero, Tulio thought.

"It's a long walk to France," said Dulce. "Wouldn't it be nice if we could go as quickly as a nose twitch?"

Then again, thought Tulio, having adventures together is nicer than being a hero alone. He nodded. "Si. It would."

"Where in France?" asked the water woman.

"Provence," he said.

"The farm where my cousin lives," Dulce added. "There's a hillside nearby, and a forest. The farm she lives on has a large meadow."

Luz smiled and waved her wand.

A moment later Tulio was in a sunny field beside a farmhouse with Dulce by his side. A few feet away another burro grazed contentedly. Two boys and a girl were chasing each other, laughing. When they saw Dulce and Tulio they stopped, wide-eyed.

The other burro looked up. "Dulce!"

"Felicia!" Dulce trotted to her cousin's side. Tulio joined them and Dulce introduced him.

"Papa! Maman!" shouted the children, as they ran up the steps and into the house.

"How did you get here so fast?" Felicia asked.

Dulce looked at Tulio. "That might take awhile to explain."

"Perhaps you would like to hear the story of Don Quixote," Tulio said.

Dulce tossed her head. "Tulio," she said, "you have your own story to tell now."

The Magic Cuckoo

"I can fly the way I am," said Eldwin, "and I already have two good friends."

Once upon a cottage in the Black Forest, there lived a German clockmaker named Horst. Horst's friend, Herr Vogel, lived in Basel, Switzerland, where he sold the cuckoo clocks Horst made.

For Herr Vogel's birthday, Horst decided to give his friend a gift. "I'll make a cuckoo clock he can keep for himself." He set off through the forest to find a good piece of wood.

In a small clearing, Horst spied a linden tree with its familiar heart shaped leaves. Not realizing the tree was magic, he cut a branch.

"Ouch," cried the branch.

Horst looked around. Seeing nothing, he shook his head and went home. Inside his house, he sat down and began to carve.

"That hurts," said the branch. Horst dropped it on the floor in fright. "That hurts too," the branch complained.

Horst shook all over. "Hush," he coaxed. "I'm carving you into a pretty bird."

"Like the birds that perched on my mother tree?" asked the branch.

"Indeed," said Horst. Pleased, the branch said nothing more. Horst quickly carved it into a cuckoo and set it before a mirror. "See how nice you look? I've even given you hinged wings that move."

The wooden bird strutted, admiring himself. He flapped his wooden wings. They clacked against his wooden body.

The cuckoo frowned. "They don't sound right."

"They are perfect for a cuckoo clock," said Horst. "Look, I am building you a little pine house." Privately he thought, He can already speak. I won't have to carve the usual pipes for his cuckoo call.

As the cuckoo watched, Horst made the house, putting a small door in the clock face. Then he built a box for the inner clockworks. He scooped the bird up and fastened its feet to a perch inside the doorway.

"What are you doing?" cried the cuckoo.

"You mustn't fall off your perch when you announce the time."

The cuckoo forgot his alarm. "Announce the time?"

"A very important job," Horst said.

The cuckoo flapped his wooden wings again with glee, then stopped. "How do I do that?" he asked.

Horst spent the rest of the day teaching the bird to cuckoo first once, then twice, then three times, and so on, until the hour of twelve.

"How will I know when to come out?" asked the bird.

"A lever will send your perch out each hour," Horst explained. He added, "You cuckoo very well."

The wooden cuckoo preened.

Horst pushed the perch and the bird inside and closed the door. Take a little nap," he called. "I'll wrap you up and send you to Herr Vogel."

In darkness, the cuckoo felt his house jiggle and jostle on a journey that seemed forever. Finally, there was a sound of ripping paper. The clock door opened. A kindly wrinkled face with bristly white brows smiled at him before the door closed again.

From his perch inside, the cuckoo heard Herr Vogel mutter, "How nice to have a cuckoo for company! Especially on rainy days like today. I'll wind the clock, and hang it just so . . ." The cuckoo heard a grinding sound of moving chains. Suddenly his house swooped upwards.

"There. Now I'll wait for one o'clock," Herr Vogel said.

The cuckoo waited too. At last there was a whirring sound. The door opened. His perch shot out.

"Cuckoo," he called, blinking in the shop's brightness. "I hope I did that right."

Herr Vogel laughed and threw up his hands. "What's this? You are a marvelous surprise!"

"Thank y—" began the cuckoo, but the perch jerked inside and the door closed. Is this all I do? he thought in the darkness.

After a long time, the lever whirred again. "Cuckoo, cuckoo," cried the wooden bird. "Can I stay out here?" Again, the perch snapped back and the door slammed. Announcing time wasn't very fun.

Through the walls, he heard Herr Vogel say, "What an unusual bird!"

"Please let me out," the cuckoo called.

Herr Vogel exclaimed, "Truly a talking cuckoo! Have no fear, little friend. I will let you out." A clinking and clanking sound below the bird's house followed. The house was in motion again. Wood splintered as the clock face was pried away.

Herr Vogel gazed kindly at the cuckoo. "Is this better, little friend?"

Little friend indeed, thought the bird. Aloud, he said, "My feet hurt."

"Ah, yes. I must remove you from your perch." The shopkeeper picked through the tools he had laid out on the counter when he removed the clock face.

After a few minutes, the cuckoo's feet were free. He flew into the air, wooden wings clacking, and landed on a grandfather clock.

Herr Vogel smiled. "You will be good company in the shop. I shall call you Eldwin, for an old friend who moved away."

Eldwin hopped down to the counter. "I want to live outside and fly in the sky, like a real cuckoo," he said.

Herr Vogel's face fell. "Oh." He sighed. "Yes. I see. Perhaps that is best. You don't belong in a clock, and you don't feel happy in a shop." Slowly the shopkeeper went to the window and opened it. "Fly away, then, but I shall miss you."

Eldwin hopped to the sill. The spring rain had lessened, but a wind blew chilly drops across his back. "It's cold out there!" he complained. If I were a real bird, my feathers would keep me warm, he thought.

Herr Vogel pulled a handkerchief from his neck and draped it over the cuckoo's back, tying the ends under the bird's chin. "Here," he said. "Maybe this will help."

Thank you," said Eldwin.

"Good-bye, little friend."

Eldwin was surprised at the heaviness in his wooden chest as he answered, "Good-bye." Just then, a flock of birds flew by overhead.

Forgetting about Herr Vogel, Eldwin decided to catch up with them. He leaped from the sill and flew into the air, but his wooden wings tipped him this way and that. Before he knew it, the flock was gone. "Maybe I'll meet other birds," he told himself.

The clouds cleared. Soon Eldwin was flying under a dazzling blue sky, over pastures edged with stone walls. A vague memory of his mother tree in the Black Forest guided him. He flew over little stands of trees and villages and farms. How tiny people looked so far below!

More birds passed Eldwin. Their curious glances embarrassed him. Enviously, he noticed their feathered wings, their sleek heads and bright eyes. They flock together, he thought. A throb of longing ran through his wooden chest. If I were a real bird I would have friends like that.

Evening came and Eldwin flapped down to a birch tree for the night. Nearby a stream gurgled. Overhead, the full moon shone milky white against the deepening blue. A sharp loneliness came over him.

"Why are you sad?" said a tinkling voice below.

At the foot of the tree a tiny winged woman stood in a ring of a red and white mushrooms. Her silky green dress glinted in the moonlight. Her pale wispy hair floated in wavelets around her face, as she hopped onto a mushroom cap. One hand rested on her pointed chin.

"Who are you?" asked Eldwin.

The little woman flew up and sat beside him. "I'm a faerie. Why are you sad?" she repeated.

"I don't have any friends," said Eldwin. "It's because I'm not a real bird," he explained. "I wish I were a real cuckoo!"

The faerie flitted three times around Eldwin's head, like a dainty green dragonfly, and sat again. "It can be done."

Eldwin's heart leapt with hope. "You can make me real?"

"You can make yourself real."

"How?"

The faerie fingered Herr Vogel's handkerchief. "This would make a nice canopy for me to sleep under," she said. "May I have it?"

"Yes, take it." Eldwin waved a wooden wing. "I have no use for it."

The faerie smiled. She untied it from his neck and folded it several times, tucking it under her arm. "When you

127

learn the meaning of true friendship," she said, "you'll become a real bird." In a flash, she darted away, disappearing into the twilight.

The growing dusk increased Eldwin's sadness. For a moment, the faerie had given him hope. He had waited for her to tell him the secret of being real. Instead, she had taken the handkerchief and left. Now he felt lonelier than ever.

A small field mouse who had heard everything scampered up the tree.

"I'll be your friend," she said. "My name is Jenell." The mouse cocked her head, her dark eyes bright.

Eldwin examined her brownish fur, her pointed nose, her whiskers. "But you're not a bird," he said.

Jenell twitched her whiskers. "Mice can be friends."

"I need to know how bird friends act if I'm going to be a real bird," said Eldwin.

Jenell fell silent. Some of her cheer seemed to disappear. After a moment she said, "I know a bird—a cuckoo, named Uta. She isn't very friendly, though."

"A cuckoo!" Eldwin gave an excited hop. "A real one?"

The mouse nodded. "She stays in that birch tree, watching a warbler's nest in those reeds."

"Why does she do that?"

"When the mother leaves," Jenell explained, "she'll lay her own egg in the nest and fly away."

"That's not nice!"

"No," Jenell agreed. "But it's what cuckoos do."

What else don't I know about cuckoos? Eldwin thought. He edged closer to the mouse. "I'd like to meet Uta."

"Carry me on your back, then. I'll introduce you."

Jenell clung to his neck as he flew to the next tree. There, a small dark bird with a long tail hunched its feathery shoulders, watching some reeds near the stream.

Jenell cleared her throat and said, "Uta, this cuckoo wants to meet you."

Uta turned around and looked Eldwin up and down. Finally, she said, "You're not a real cuckoo." She went back to peering at the reeds.

"I'll be real when I learn about friendship," Eldwin protested. Uta didn't answer.

"Let's go back," whispered Jenell.

His chest aching, Eldwin returned to his tree. "I'll never get to be a real cuckoo," he said.

Jenell hopped off his back. She twitched her whiskers. "I like you the way you are." She scampered down the tree, and disappeared into a hole next to the faerie ring of mushrooms.

In spite of his disappointment, Eldwin felt his wooden chest grow warm. That was nice of her, he thought, and he drifted off to sleep.

The next morning Eldwin woke up, excited by an idea: If he gave Uta a gift, she would want to be his friend.

He flew to the ground. The air was clear and crisp; the sun was bright. Eldwin looked around, this way and that. What would please a real cuckoo?

Jenell peeked out of her burrow. "Can I help you find something?"

"I'm looking for a gift for Uta," Eldwin replied. Suddenly he spied a beautiful yellow feather. "This is perfect. Uta can use this to decorate her nest."

"It's a finch feather and very pretty," said Jenell, "but cuckoos don't have nests of their own." She eyed the feather wistfully.

Eldwin was too excited to listen. He snatched the feather in his beak and flew to the branch where Uta sat, still watching the reeds. Laying the feather next to her, Eldwin said, "This is for you."

Uta turned. She looked coldly at the yellow feather— and at him.

"I have no use for that," she said. Just then, the warbler rose from the reeds with a whir of gray wings and flew away. Uta swept down, to take her place.

130

Eldwin picked up the finch feather and flew to his own birch tree. Jenell scampered up to sit beside him.

Eldwin put the feather down, hanging his head. "She didn't want it."

The mouse patted his wing with a tiny paw. "Don't feel bad. It's still a beautiful gift."

Eldwin looked at Jenell, thinking of her kindness. "Would you like to have it?" he asked.

"Oh!" Jenell exclaimed. "It will look so pretty in my burrow." She picked it up in her teeth and ran down the tree to her hole.

A moment later she returned, her eyes gleaming. "I put it right inside the entrance," she said, "so that it glows in the sunlight."

How nice it felt to have his gift appreciated. "I'm glad you like it," he said shyly. A memory of Herr Vogel's handkerchief flickered through his thoughts: That was a gift.

Then a cuckoo call from the reeds caught Eldwin's attention and the notion vanished. A moment later, Uta flew back up to her branch, only to push off the branch again and fly away.

"Wait!" Eldwin called. Already her soaring figure had grown smaller in the distance. "Now I'll never learn about friendship," he told Jenell. "Now I'll never get to be a real bird."

"We're friends," she pointed out.

"What good is that?" Elwin cried. "I need to learn about bird friendship."

The light in Jenell's eyes faded. With a flick of her tail, she ran down the tree and disappeared into her burrow.

How empty the tree limb seemed! Eldwin shifted back and forth on his wooden feet, hoping the mouse would come back, but she didn't.

The day wore on, and still Eldwin sat alone. His thoughts skittered this way and that. They kept coming back to Jenell's disappointed face.

"She didn't mind that I'm only a wooden bird," he muttered to himself. "She appreciated my present. She tried to cheer me up when I felt bad."

He stared down at the mouse-hole next to the ring of mushrooms. Maybe I can't be a real cuckoo, he thought, but I can be a real friend. He flapped down to the burrow's entrance.

"Jenell?" he called. Deep inside the burrow's darkness, he thought he saw a gleam of eyes. "I'm sorry," he said. "I want to be your friend."

A moment later, Jenell was in the entrance. She patted Eldwin's wing with her tiny paw.

"Friendship is friendship," he told her.

A tinkling sound made them both look over at the mushroom circle. The little green faerie sat cross-legged on a red mushroom cap. She rose and flitted over to them.

"Greetings," she said in her tiny, musical voice.

Eldwin noticed Herr Vogel's handkerchief was still folded under her arm. A pang went through him, seeing the shopkeeper's gift: Herr Vogel had liked him even though he was a wooden bird. Herr Vogel had tried to make him happy by letting him fly away.

"May I have that handkerchief back?" Eldwin asked the faerie. "I need to return to Herr Vogel and thank him."

"What?" asked the faerie. "I thought you wanted to be a real cuckoo so you could have friends. Are you giving up so soon?"

"I can fly the way I am," said Eldwin, "and I already have two good friends."

Smiling, the faerie gave him the handkerchief. "It looks like they have a true friend, too."

Eldwin turned to Jenell. "I must go back and let Herr Vogel know I'm his friend. But I'll come back to visit, I promise."

Jenell nodded. She twitched her nose and said, "I'll think of you whenever I see my finch feather."

Eldwin held the handkerchief in his beak and rose into the air. All night long he flew, eager to see the shopkeeper. In the morning, when he reached the shop, the window was open. A warm glow started in Eldwin's chest and began to spread all through him. He lit on the sill, peering inside. Herr Vogel was dusting clocks on the wall.

Eldwin dropped the handkerchief on the sill and folded his wings. To his surprise, they made no noise. Glancing at them, he found they were covered with feathers.

"Good morning, Herr Vogel," he called.

The shopkeeper turned. His bristly brows nearly went to his hairline. Coming to the window, he stared at the handkerchief, then at Eldwin.

"Eldwin," he said, stroking the cuckoo's feathered head. "Is that you?"

"I missed you, my good friend," said Eldwin.

The Contest of Surprises

Monsieur Trotter exclaimed, "What lovely birds!" Pakrit spread his
tail even wider.

Once upon a princely state in northern India, Pakrit Peacock strutted with his two friends in the royal courtyard. The Maharajah was showing visitors around the palace grounds.

"My tail's eye-spots outshine the sapphires in the Maharajah's turban," Pakrit told himself. He spread his splendid tail to command attention. Instead, everyone looked up.

A brightly patterned hot air balloon floated above the tamarind trees edging the courtyard. A man with a twirly mustache peered from the wicker basket that hung below the balloon. Pakrit watched him drop an anchor, hooking it on a branch. The man tugged the basket to the ground and tied it to the tree. Stepping out, he bowed to the Maharajah.

"Bonjour," he said. "My name is Monsieur Trotteur. I have come all the way from Paris." Spying the peafowls, he exclaimed, "What lovely birds!"

Pakrit spread his tail even wider.

The Maharajah smiled. "My humble attempt at a bird park. They have harsh voices, though." He eyed the deflating balloon. "Do many of your countrymen travel this way?"

"Many have tried, Your Highness," said Monsieur Trotteur. "None have come this far. Would you like a ride?"

The Maharajah laughed. "I prefer to stay on the ground." He straightened his blue and green embroidered jacket. "I was just giving a tour of the grounds. Will you join us?" He led the group and Monsieur Trotteur past a fountain to a stand of neem trees on the other side of the courtyard.

Pakrit and his friends lingered, watching the balloon turn to folds of crumpled silk.

"I would like to go up in that balloon," said Saloni, a small blue peahen with a speckled tail.

"Who wants to sit in that silly basket?" scoffed Pakrit.

"We can fly without it," Vijay agreed.

His words stirred Pakrit's jealousy: Vijay could fly higher than most peacocks, all the way to the top of the seven-level courtyard fountain. To change the subject, Pakrit said, "Let's go listen to what the Maharajah is saying."

The fragrance of neem blossoms and jasmine wafted to him as they neared the group. Beyond the neem trees, hummingbirds hovered over red pomegranate flowers.

"Stay a few days," the Maharajah was telling the Frenchman. "I shall have three peafowl contests for your pleasure: tail-spreading, running, and flying. For now, let us return to the palace to enjoy the feast my servants have prepared."

The peafowls ran back to the fountain, their long tail feathers trailing the ground.

"I'll win the tail-spread contest," Pakrit boasted. He looked over his shoulder and once again fanned his tail.

"Vijay will win the flying contest," said Saloni.

Pakrit closed his tail and ruffled his wings. "People admire peacocks for their tails," he reminded her.

"Forget these silly contests. I'm hungry," she said. She ran to mango grove beyond the pomegranate trees where small lizards and mice could be found. Pakrit and Vijay followed.

The next morning, the Maharajah strode out to the courtyard, followed by servants and surrounded by guests, including Monsieur Trotteur. He called the gamekeeper over. The peafowls drew near.

"Tomorrow," the Maharajah announced, "I will hold four peafowl contests, not three. The winners of the first three will have royal meals for a week. The fourth contest shall be . . ." He folded his arms. Everyone waited. ". . . the Contest of Surprises. The bird that delights me with the most interesting surprise will become my Royal Peafowl. It will wear a golden necklace and have royal meals for the rest of its life."

"Splendide!" said Monsieur Trotteur.

"Practice with the birds today," The Maharajah told the gamekeeper in a low voice. Turning to his guests with a grand sweep of his hands, he said, "This morning, for your amusement, I have arranged a game of croquet. This afternoon we shall have elephant rides."

Pakrit's thoughts raced as he watched the Maharajah and his guests disappear down the path for their game. Royal Peacock! What could he do to surprise the Maharajah?

The gamekeeper coached Pakrit and Vijay as they practiced their tail-spreads. Saloni watched, since her peahen tail was too short and dull to attract any notice. Pakrit raised his tail higher and higher, fanning it out. He shook it to make the eye spots glisten in the sunlight.

"You will win this contest," Saloni called. Pakrit's chest swelled with pride.

They practiced running next. Saloni outran both peacocks.

Then came flying. Pakrit beat his wings frantically, but he could only reach the third tier of the fountain. Vijay flew to the top level.

"Wonderful," cried Saloni, and Pakrit felt a knot in his throat.

Noon came. The sun beat down. The gamekeeper wiped his forehead. "We will continue after lunch," he said. He set off for the servants' quarters. Vijay and Saloni went off in different directions.

Pakrit paced back and forth in the courtyard, racking his brain. "What can I do for a surprise?" he muttered. "What will the others do? If I know that, maybe I can outsmart them."

He sneaked over to the neem trees, where he saw Saloni, standing motionless, her head high. Pretending to look for worms, Pakrit watched from the corner of his eye. Saloni stepped to the left; she stepped to the right; she hopped.

Some kind of a dance!

He walked on down to the pomegranate trees, desperate for ideas. An excited cry from Saloni made him turn. She was looking up, craning her long beautiful neck: Vijay was flying above one of the neem trees. No. More than flying! He was doing circles and loops!

Pakrit felt a heavy lump in his gizzard. He ran to the mango trees and down a long path to the small lake on the other side. Stopping to rest under a tree, he stared at the bamboo edging the lake. Half a day had gone by, and he was the only one with no surprise for the Maharajah.

Musical whistling from a nearby bush interrupted his thoughts. How sweet it sounded! The voice trilled and peeped in a lilting tune, like a song whistled by a human. Pakrit looked closer. A small blue bird with a darker blue head peered back at him—a Malabar whistling-thrush. Normally they whistled at dawn.

"Why are you whistling at noon?" Pakrit asked him.

The thrush puffed out his chest. "I, Mitali, like to stand out from others." He bobbed his head. "And why do you look heavy-hearted on such a fine afternoon?"

Pakrit sighed. "I must win a contest if I want to become the Maharajah's Royal Peacock."

The thrush hopped to the ground. "But, you have such a beautiful tail! Of course you will win!" He gave a cheery whistle that sounded like, have no fear, be of good cheer.

"It isn't a tail contest that worries me," said Pakrit. He told the small blue thrush about the Contest of Surprises.

"What are the other peafowls doing?" Mitali asked.

Pakrit frowned. "Vijay can fly loops; Saloni is doing a dance."

"Hmm," said Mitali. "Then you must sing a song. Humans like songs. I'll teach you." He burst into his beautiful whistling again. "Now you try," he said.

Pakrit tried. His usual harsh piercing cry came out. Even Mitali shuddered.

"It's no use," said Pakrit.

"Wait, my friend," said Mitali. He cocked his head. "I have an idea. But if I help you win, will you share your royal food with me for the rest of your life?"

"Of course," said Pakrit. "I'll give you a little bit each day."

"No," said Mitali. "I want half of what you get every day."

"That's too much," Pakrit protested. Then he pictured Vijay becoming the Royal Peacock. Saloni would admire Vijay instead of him. "All right," he agreed. "But no one must know." Remembering his own spying on Saloni, he peered over his shoulder to see if anyone had followed him.

"Here is my idea," Mitali said. I'll hide under your wing and sing. No one will notice if my feathers show; they are the same blue as your own." He hopped to Pakrit's back and crawled under his wing.

Pakrit shifted from foot to foot. "How is it?" he finally asked.

"Dark," said Mitali. But he burst into a whistle, and the beautiful notes floated out into the air.

Pakrit raised his wing. "Wonderful," he cried.

They worked out a signal: Pakrit would open his beak; then he would press his wing to his side, and Mitali would begin his song. When Pakrit pressed his wing again, Mitali would stop.

"I'll watch the first three contests from a tree nearby," suggested Mitali. "When no one's looking, lift your wing, and I'll fly under it."

Pakrit returned to his friends smiling to himself. How astonished everyone will be when I open my beak and Mitali's song fills the air. Not even Vijay's loops can be as surprising as that, he thought.

The following morning everyone gathered in the courtyard. Servants with fans stood behind the guests. The Maharajah sat on his special ivory chair carved like lace.

The gamekeeper came forward and bowed. "Your Highness, we are ready. First, the tail-spread." He signaled to the two peacocks and they strutted into the courtyard, fanning and flourishing their tails.

Pakrit fluttered his tail slowly at first. He let it tremble and shake, drawing it higher, fanning it wider. He glanced to one side: Vijay's tail spread wasn't nearly as full.

"C'est superbe," said the Frenchman, pointing at Pakrit's tail. Pakrit fanned it even wider, until the Maharajah declared him the winner.

Saloni joined them next. They lined up in front of the mango grove in the stretch between the neem trees and the fountain. At the game keeper's signal, the birds ran to the far side of the courtyard. Pakrit and Vijay huffed and puffed, but soon Saloni pulled ahead and came in first.

As Pakrit had expected, Vijay won the flying contest.

The Maharajah raised a hand to quiet the applause. "It is time for the Contest of Surprises," he announced.

The game keeper bowed once more, waving Saloni forward. She also bowed and then was still for a moment. On a count of three, she began: step-step-step to the right, hop-hop-hop; step-step-step to the left, hop-hop-hop. Cries of pleasure ran around the audience. When she finished her dance, everyone cheered.

Vijay was next. He, too, bowed to the Maharajah. Pakrit watched from under the mango tree he and Mitali had agreed on. His throat tightened. If Vijay won, it wouldn't be from tricks.

Vijay sailed high, into his loops. All eyes were upon him. Pakrit lifted a wing and Mitali darted under it.

When Vijay finished three grand circles and three soaring loops, the Frenchman shouted, "Magnifique!" Everyone clapped until it seemed their arms would fall off.

"Next?" said the Maharajah, with a sweep of his hand.

Pakrit's legs trembled as he walked out and bowed. He opened his beak and pressed his wing to his side, and the thrush began to whistle. The look of shock on the Maharajah's face thrilled Pakrit and made him forget his guilt. He opened and closed his beak, over and over, and the thrush whistled on. Finally, Pakrit pressed his wing against his side, and the whistling stopped.

For a moment, no one spoke. Then the air exploded with applause and voices.

The Maharajah rose and waved for silence. "Never have I heard of such a thing," he said. "A peacock that can whistle a song!" He came forward, holding the golden chain Pakrit wanted. "You have earned this, noble bird," he said, hanging the chain around Pakrit's neck.

Unable to contain his excitement, Pakrit flapped his wings for joy, and out fell the little thrush. Quickly Mitali scrambled to his feet. A titter of laughter ran around the guests. At the Maharajah's outraged scowl, a new silence fell over the courtyard.

"What is this!" the Maharajah asked in a terrible voice. Pakrit felt his gizzard turn to ice. Mitali took wing and soared out of sight.

The Maharajah reached over and removed the golden chain from Pakrit's neck. He placed it over Vijay's head.

"You are truly a noble and faithful bird," he said. "Your honest surprise gave us much pleasure."

The Maharajah turned to Pakrit. "And you . . ."

Pakrit trembled from the crest on his head to the talons on his feet. His beak opened and closed, but this time not a sound came out.

"Chop off his head," the Maharajah told the gamekeeper.

Monsieur Trotteur approached the Maharajah. "Excuse me Your Highness; I have another idea. Why not banish him?"

"That is no punishment!" the Maharajah scoffed.

"Ah, Your Highness," said the Frenchman, "it is no small thing to lose your country. I can take him to the aviary at the Jardin des Plantes, in Paris. He will think on this shame for the rest of his life. And," Monsieur Trotteur

147

added, "it will be a nice present to the French government. A gift from Your Highness would please them."

The Maharajah clasped his hands behind him, pacing back and forth. "Yes," he finally said. "He will be punished, and I will have good relations with France."

He beckoned to the gamekeeper. "Lock the cheater up until tomorrow morning when Monsieur Trotteur leaves." To the guests, he said, "Let us return to the palace for a last banquet with our visitor from France."

Morning arrived. Pakrit sat in the wicker basket, watching Monsieur Trotteur light a small fire. The Frenchman worked the bellows, pumping hot air into the colorful balloon. Pakrit turned his head and saw his friends regarding him with accusing stares. Saloni shook her head. Pakrit quickly looked away.

Monsieur Trotteur freed the anchor from the tree and pulled it into the basket. The balloon began to rise. A gust of wind caught them up. Cool air rushed through the ropes that held the basket secure. Pakrit looked over the basket's edge. The Maharajah, his guests, and the peafowls were all becoming specks.

Tears ran from his eyes. Gone were the days when he would strut with his friends in the courtyard. Or hear the tinkling fountain. Or smell the sweet scent of jasmine and neem blossoms in the warm evening air. Or hope for a gleam of admiration in Saloni's eyes.

The Piano Lesson

Marmion leapt to the chandelier, where he swung, a grin on his little monkey face.

O nce upon a Paris parlor, Jolie and Noel sat sulking. Jolie twiddled her fingers on the keys of the upright piano. Noel slumped in a high-backed chair. Tante Suzette, their father's sister, peered out the open window. The April breeze stirred the leaves of the potted fern next to her.

"Such a pretty day," she said.

"And we have to stay inside and practice," Noel complained. If only he could run to the corner and see Marmion, the organ grinder's monkey. Marmion would tip his hat, somersault, and bow, all for three centimes.

"And we have to play scales in twelve different keys," Jolie said. "Five times each!"

Tante Suzette walked over and patted Jolie's shoulder. "As your Maman says, one must practice to play well."

153

Normally Maman oversaw their practice. But now she came to the hall doorway, wearing her bonnet and cloak. She tied the bonnet's sash beneath her chin and smiled, her cheeks dimpling. "I'm off to get your papa's birthday present," she said. "Tante Suzette will listen to your scales."

"I have to go shopping too," their aunt protested.

"We could supervise each other," Jolie said. She pictured herself folding her hands, nodding, the way Maman did, and reminding Noel to keep time better.

Noel sat up and grinned. His blue eyes brightened. "Oui, we can supervise each other."

Maman's brow puckered.

"They will do an excellent job," cried Tante Suzette, who seemed to have forgotten their earlier scowls. "Such a big boy and girl," she added, adjusting the bustle of her walking dress. She hurried from the room to get her cloak and bonnet, before Maman could refuse.

"Promise you will play every scale," Maman said.

"I promise." Noel nodded with so much enthusiasm she gave him a sharp look.

"Every single scale," Jolie assured her.

"Very well." Maman relaxed into a smile. "And then practice the duet you're going to play for your papa tonight after dinner. Remember," she wagged a finger, "'La Poupée' is a sweet lullaby, not a march."

She blew each of them a kiss and went into the hall, where Tante Suzette joined her. The hall carpet muffled the women's steps, but a moment later Jolie and Noel heard the heavy front door open, then shut with a thud and a click.

"I'll start," said Jolie. She set the upside-down pendulum of the wooden metronome to ticking and began.

Noel hurried to the open window and peeked out. His mother and aunt were climbing into a hansom cab. The driver flicked the reins and the horse set off. At the corner, Monsieur Bouchard stood, hands on hips, craning his neck this way and that and shouting. It sounded like he was yelling "Marmion." His beret was askew on his dark shaggy hair. His box organ hung from a strap on his neck. The monkey was nowhere in sight.

Jolie finished her scale with a chord. "That was once." She began again.

Noel drew his head inside and ambled to the piano. "I'm not going to play each scale five times." He stopped the ticking pendulum of the little wooden box.

Jolie set it ticking again. "Yes. You are."

"You can't make me," he taunted, as she resumed her scale.

"You promised," she said. "But we can take turns to make it more interesting. When I get to five, you can play."

When it was his turn, he pounded the keys to show his annoyance.

"I'm counting," Jolie reminded him.

He hurried through the next scale.

"You aren't even following the metronome," she said, exasperated. "Slow down!"

He purposely played the next ver-r-r-y slow.

"Don't be like that," she said.

When it was her turn again, right away Noel hissed, "I'm counting."

"Don't be angry," she coaxed. "You know Maman can read our faces. She'll see right away we didn't practice. And then we will be in so much trouble with Papa."

What a dull afternoon it was, Noel fumed. Taking turns didn't help. Giving little flourishes on the ending chords didn't help. Sitting side by side supervising each other didn't help, either. Jolie was worse than Maman.

So intent were they on overseeing each other, neither saw the small monkey face at the window. Marmion climbed in and sat on the sill, listening. He lifted his little red beret with one hand and rubbed the dark hair above his pale face with the other.

Noel had just finished his last scale, and Jolie had opened the collection of twelve duets to the page for "La Poupée," when Marmion jumped on the fern. The tall brass urn teetered and fell with a clanging bump that made both Jolie and Noel fairly fly off the bench. They spun around in time to see the monkey leap to the nearest chair, chattering wildly.

Jolie giggled. "It's Marmion! Come here, you naughty creature!" But Marmion climbed atop the chair's back.

"What a mess," said Noel. Dirt was scattered under the window. The fern's fronds spread crookedly on the parquet wood at the carpet edge. They set the urn upright and straightened the fern, then scooped up remaining dirt clumps, patting them around the base of the plant. They flicked the last traces under the carpet. Marmion watched from his perch, eyes glittering.

"There's a dent," cried Jolie. "They'll think we were playing games instead of scales!" She rubbed the urn's metal rim, as if her finger might smooth the mark away.

Noel scratched his head, making his hair stand up in tufts. "Let's turn it," he decided. Carefully they twisted the metal pot making the dent face the window.

Outside, Monsieur Bouchard's shouts could be heard as he came up the street: "Misery-maker! Imitation of a monkey! Where are you?"

157

Marmion made a clucking sound from the chair. Noel quickly closed the window.

Jolie gave a contented sigh. "Here he is, right in our parlor," she told Noel. "Let's put him through all his tricks. Tip your hat, Marmion," she said. Right away the monkey raised his beret. He fingered a button on his red jacket.

Noel's eyes grew round. "Let's teach him to play the piano!"

"What a brilliant idea!" Jolie said. "Come here, Marmion," she cooed. "Come and get your piano lesson." Marmion hopped to the next chair.

"Turn a somersault, Marmion," Noel called. The monkey somersaulted to the floor, and his red beret fell off.

"Grab him," said Jolie. But Marmion ran to the piano bench, and they grabbed each other instead. Marmion hopped next to the top of the piano then leapt to the chandelier, where he swung, a grin on his little monkey face.

Jolie picked up Marmion's beret, then reached up and gently grabbed his tail. When he tried to snatch his tail back, she waved the beret at him. After a pause, Marmion dropped to her shoulder.

"Look Noel, he likes me."

"I'm sure he likes me too," Noel said, put out.

"Marmion," Jolie said, "we are going to give you a piano lesson. We'll teach you to play scales. We are very good scale players."

"Give him to me, I'll teach him," Noel said.

"No, I'll teach him."

"I'm the oldest."

"But I play better scales," Jolie said, "because I don't cheat."

Noel flushed. "I didn't cheat."

"Only because I wouldn't let you."

"We have to take turns with him, just like we did with the scales. Give him to me."

"But not short turns," Jolie said. "We'll count to five. One hundred, two hundred," she began very slowly.

"One-two-three-four-five, he's mine." Noel snatched the monkey from her and carried him to the bench. "I will give you your first lesson," he said. "Pay attention."

The monkey put his hand to his mouth and stifled a sound Jolie could almost swear was a laugh. They seated themselves with the monkey between them.

"Hold him," said Noel. "I'll show him what to do."

"You should let me show him. You don't keep proper time."

"One-two-three-four-five, he's yours now." Noel thrust the monkey at her and placed his hands on the piano

159

keys. "Watch, Marmion," he said. "This is the key of C major." He began pounding the keys.

Jolie sighed. "I will give you a correct lesson when he's finished," she told the monkey.

But Marmion wriggled free from her arms, stood up, and began examining the book of duets propped against the music rack. He leaned forward, thumbing through the score of "La Poupée" with great attention.

Jolie gasped. Noel stopped playing. Both stared at the monkey and then at each other.

"He can't read music," Noel said in a whisper. "Can he?"

Jolie licked her lips nervously. "It seems he can," she whispered back.

Marmion straightened the lapels of his little red jacket. He sat back down and then stretched across both their laps, resting his head on Jolie's and his back feet on Noel's.

"How sweet," Jolie was going to say, as the monkey rolled on his side, but the words stuck in her throat. Marmion was starting to rise in the air, balancing on his tail, which angled below as if it were a strong pole. When he was level with the piano keys, he stretched out his hands and feet, and began to play "La Poupée."

With his feet playing Noel's part and his hands playing Jolie's, the duet sounded like the lullaby it was supposed to be. Occasionally, Marmion closed his eyes, giving himself up to notes that seemed a murmured musical conversation, a dreamy smile on his wizened face. Spellbound, Jolie and Noel realized for the first time what a pretty lullaby it was. Until now, it had just been one more thing to practice, with their elbows getting in the way.

When he finished, he lowered himself to the bench, stood, and bowed, while they continued to gape, speechless.

A heavy rap from the front door's metal knocker roused them out of their shock.

"Wait here," Noel cautioned. He rose and went to the window, raising it. The organ grinder stood outside the door, a forlorn look on his face. He turned and spied Noel.

"Bon jour," he said.

Noel ducked his head inside. "It's Monsieur Bouchard."

"You'll have to open the door," Jolie said. They gave each other a long look.

"First, we should hide him," Noel said.

"I don't know . . ."

"He can teach us more of the duets. Take him to my room."

"It should be my room," she said immediately. "Yours is too messy."

"My room," Noel insisted.

Marmion leapt in the air again. Hanging by his tail from the chandelier, he began swinging back and forth.

The metal knocker rapped again.

"You'll have to let him in," Jolie said. "Think of something to say."

Noel went into the hallway, and a moment later she heard him say, "Monsieur Bouchard!" as if he was ever so surprised.

"Marmion, come down from there," Jolie hissed. The monkey shook his head.

"Merci, thank you." The organ grinder's voice floated down the hall. "I will just leave my box organ out on the step." The door closed. "Have you been outside today?"

Noel cleared his throat. "Non."

Jolie felt a twinge of guilt. She tiptoed to the hall doorway and stood just inside, listening. Marmion kept swinging from the chandelier.

"I hoped one of you had seen my monkey," said the organ grinder. "He has disappeared. Sometimes he plays games with me. He is such a smart fellow."

Marmion stopped swinging and bared his teeth in a monkey smile, as Jolie returned to coax him down.

"Actually," Noel began.

"He hides," said Monsieur Bouchard, more talkative than Jolie had ever heard him. "When I take him off his chain, he'll hide behind a flower stand, or under one of the outside café tables or chairs. I pretend not to see him. I call and call, then — voilà! — there he is!" The organ grinder heaved a sigh. "But today, no voilà. He's gone. My heart is broken."

Marmion looked as sad as Monsieur Bouchard sounded. He let go of the chandelier with his tail, dropping to Jolie's shoulder. She hugged him tightly.

"Well, er, Monsieur . . . actually . . ."

"Marmion," Jolie whispered, "if we give you back, will you come and teach us again?"

The monkey nodded.

"All of the duets in that book?"

Another nod.

"Do you promise?"

He gave her a crafty smile.

"We'll give you a treat," she said. When he nodded again, she said, "Very well."

Still hugging him, she came into the hall. "Actually, Monsieur, here he is—voilà!" Marmion broke into excited cheeps, stretching his arms out to the organ grinder.

Noel made a fierce face at her.

163

With a cry, Monsieur Bouchard grabbed the monkey and clasped him close.

Jolie mouthed to Noel, "He wanted to go home."

"Marmion! Mon cher, mon petit chou," Monsieur Bouchard crooned, repeating, over and over, "my dear, my little cabbage."

"Marmion is so smart," Jolie told him. "We had no idea how smart he was until . . ." (Marmion put a finger to his lips.) ". . . he did his tricks for us."

Monsieur Bouchard held Marmion high in the air. "Oui, you are so smart, mon chou."

Noel said, "Actually he can . . ." (Marmion shook his head ever so slightly.) ". . . swing from the chandelier by his tail."

"I hope he was no trouble." When they both shook their heads, Monsieur Bouchard said, "I must get back to my spot on the corner." He gave Marmion a severe look. "I lost business today over your absence, rascal!" He tipped his black beret to the twins as he went out the door. "Adieu." Peeking over his shoulder, Marmion tipped his red beret and winked.

Jolie closed the door. "Marmion has promised to come back and teach us to play all twelve duets," she told Noel.

Still in a state of wonder, they wandered back into the parlor and sat on the bench. Slowly, they put their hands on the keys, this time without jostling or complaining.

"I think he began very softly, like this," Jolie said.

As they played the opening passages of "La Poupèe," the front door opened, and their mother and aunt came in.

"What did you get Papa?" Noel asked Maman.

"A pocket watch he has wanted." Flushing with pleasure, Maman took the gold watch from her handbag and brought it over to show them the black roman numerals circling its face.

"And I found your papa this elegant watch fob," Tante Suzette said, holding up a jeweled clip to attach to the watch chain.

"How did the practice go?" asked Maman.

"We played every single scale," Noel said.

"We were just starting on 'La Poupèe'," added Jolie. "It really is so pretty. Shall we play it for you?"

The two women sat and listened while they played it all the way through. When they finished, Maman said, in a wondering voice, "How beautiful that was! You've captured the way it should sound."

"Oui," agreed Tante Suzette. "We can leave them to supervise each other again."

Noel and Jolie exchanged secretive smiles.

"We had better go wrap your papa's presents before he gets home," Maman said. "But I am proud of you both. Aren't you, Suzette?"

Seeing her mother and aunt so pleased, Jolie began to worry about when they would find the dent on the brass urn.

"Maman," she began, "I know a monkey who likes to play piano."

Noel nudged her.

Tante Suzette tweaked Jolie's nose, then tousled Noel's hair.

"I know two monkeys who like to play piano," she told Maman, and they left the room, still laughing as they went up the hall.

The Lost Tail

"Up ye go" said the sprite and he snapped his fingers to make Digger
visible again as the dinosaur hopped onto the box-like table.

O nce upon a Midsummer's Eve—a magical time, when even bones have memories—a dinosaur skeleton stood upright on his box-like plinth in London's British Museum of Natural History. How long he had been there, he didn't know. The museum warder was reading his information card to a woman and a small boy.

"Dinosaurus Fossurus sine Cauda. That's Latin for 'Digger Dinosaur without a Tail'," he explained. "We call him Digger. His three-toed front feet were for digging roots. You can see he was about the size of a collie dog. Fast, too. Those long back legs were for running and jumping."

The little boy giggled. "He looks funny without a tail."

After they left, Digger brooded over the boy's laughter. Through the mist of time, he remembered running from a huge beast with hot breath that wanted to eat him. He also remembered twitching a long tail as he ran.

Sadness swept through Digger's bones. I want my tail back, he thought.

At this moment, in a Cornish village many miles from London, a naughty green sprite named Puck was thinking up tricks. Puck could work magic, especially on Midsummer's Eve. Each year the villagers made bonfires and danced in circles. Sometimes Puck snapped his tiny green fingers and made them dance with donkeys or climb trees or bark like dogs.

New mischief needs new inspiration, Puck thought. Maybe I'll try a big city like London this year. He spied a crow on a nearby tree branch, spreading its wings for take-off. "Plague of farmers, can ye take me to London?" Puck asked.

The bird cawed, "Too far. But I can take ye part way, and others can take ye further."

Puck climbed on and soon was high in the air, the breeze rushing past his ears. Buildings below looked like small pebbles. Trees looked like bits of clover.

After the crow landed and said goodbye, Puck saw another crow pecking crumbs on the village green. "Omen of bad tidings, can ye take me to London?" he asked.

"Too far," said the crow. "But I'll take ye part way and others can do the rest."

Three crows later, Puck was pleased to see a grand city spread beneath him. The crow flew lower, circling a tall tower that ended in a sharp peak. A huge clock face was on each side of the tower.

Puck clapped his tiny green hands. "What a fine building!"

Hardly had he said that when the bell inside the tower rang out in deep, echoing tones.

"That's Big Ben," the crow cawed.

"The building has a name?"

"Big Ben is the bell," the crow explained.

Below, horse hooves clopped on cobblestones. Carriage wheels clattered. Voices jabbered. Twilight turned the evening blue. Gas street lamps pulsed with yellow light.

"What a hubbub of noise and color be London," Puck exclaimed.

The crow landed on the roof of an ivy-covered tavern.

"Stay here, and I will see you are well rewarded for bringing me here," said Puck. He climbed down the ivy. Then he made himself invisible and waited at the tavern door until a two-wheeled hansom cab pulled up. The driver got down and tied his horse to a pole.

171

Puck smiled, snapping his invisible fingers, and the man began to dance a jig. He danced into the tavern. A few minutes later he danced out again with a meat pasty. Still hopping and kicking, he threw it into the air, and the crow swooped by and snatched it.

Puck chortled, rubbing his hands together. "Ah, 'tis a fine place for mischief I find myself in!" he called after the crow.

He wandered around London for quite some time, watching people. Vendors called their wares from stalls. Street urchins begged on corners, or ran into narrow alleys. Men and women strolled the avenues, arm in arm. The men wore top hats. Puck made one hat fall off and roll down the street. The man chased after it. The women wore dresses with bustles and hats with feathers and flowers. Puck made a bunch of flowers come loose and fly away. How he laughed to see the woman's companion trying to catch it.

Then Puck came to a huge building on the corner. Its wide stone steps led up to two arched doors under an alcove with pillars.

Here's a grand place, Puck thought, and he chanted,

"Open doors and open wide;

I will have a look inside."

Soon Puck was skipping along the mosaic tile floor in the main hall of the British Museum of Natural History. He

172

paused at a large skeleton whose bones sent him the idea of an ocean. Puck strained his brain some more. Wavelets of pride floated down from the huge bony figure: Sperm whale.

What be a Sperm whale? Puck wondered. He continued down the hall. At last he reached the small room where Digger stood on his plinth.

Puck had learned to read in many languages a few hundred years ago. "Dinosaurus Fossurus sine Cauda," he read aloud. "Digger dinosaur without a tail."

A sparkle of thoughts and feelings sprinkled over Puck, like dust motes. He caught a sense of sorrow from the small bony figure—something about a tail.

Puck concentrated. At last he understood the source of the dinosaur's sadness. An idea seized the little sprite that made him turn three somersaults from excitement. He knew how he would entertain himself this night! Immediately he made himself visible to the skeleton.

"Digger," he said, "I think ye be right about that tail."

Surprise sprinkled down from the dinosaur's bones.

"Tonight, at the magic hour of midnight," said Puck, "I'll restore ye to yer old self, and we'll go looking for that tail. In the morning, won't the museum warder have a fine surprise waiting for him!" The sprite sat cross-legged on the wooden floor and waited.

A few minutes before twelve, he began to sing:

173

"Come you head and have new eyes;

Tonight we find a wanted prize.

Grow you muscle, skin and scale;

Tonight we find a missing tail."

He sang the song three times.

Outside, Big Ben tolled the hour. Puck snapped his little green fingers at the skeleton. "Come alive," he whispered.

Slowly Digger's bones became covered with muscle and gray leathery skin. As Puck watched, purple scales grew over the skin, starting from the dinosaur's toes and ending at his tapering jaws. Two round, lidded eyes filled in what had been empty eye sockets. The small dinosaur craned his neck to get a better look at the green sprite below.

"Come with me," said Puck.

Digger wagged the small stump—all that remained of his missing tail. His back feet thudded on the wooden floor when he hopped down. He followed Puck down the hallway to the main hall, his clawed feet going clickety-click on the tiles as they passed the sperm whale skeleton. At the entrance doors Puck chanted:

"Open doors and open wide;

We must find a tail outside."

Then they were outside on a street where a carriage rattled along the cobblestones.

Puck made himself and the dinosaur invisible to everyone but each other. He hopped onto the dinosaur's back. "Let yer bones remember where ye left yer tail," he told Digger, "and off we'll go."

Digger had been a fast runner when he was alive, and soon they were far outside the city of London, traveling through trees and brush. A three-quarter moon hung bright in the sky, lighting pastures below. They passed brooks and stands of trees; then orchards; then forests; then fields divided by low stone walls.

Everything is so different, thought Digger. Even the sky! In spite of his confusion, he followed what felt like a call from stones under the fields. Finally, he came to the banks of a small river. He waded into it. It felt like the same water he remembered. He waded deeper. It was the same river, but not as wide. He waded to the other side.

"Ye think yer tail's somewhere along the Thames River?" asked Puck.

Digger stopped and snuffed at the night air. A keen scent assailed his nostrils.

"Willow bark," Puck guessed, catching the sparkly thoughts.

Digger peered again at the landscape around him. Plants, trees, bushes, and the river. There was more of everything when he was alive. The plants were different. There were no people. Only flowing waters, endless green, and a cool dark cave. An ache throbbed inside him as he crept along the riverbank, trying to feel the message of underground stones. Images came to him: Bones. Fear. Running. He stopped. Snorting softly with excitement, he began to push aside brambles and tall grasses.

"Hah!" cried Puck. "Think ye've found the place, do ye?"

Digger picked around roots. He lifted rocks and dug below them. Then he hesitated and stood erect, baffled. No, this wasn't quite the place.

A memory flashed through him: Running through the woods, hoping to reach his cave. Again, he was scrambling up a tree, leaping into the water he had just waded through. Again, he could hear the beast splash behind him as he swam across the river. Just when he had reached the cave's entrance, the beast pounced on his long tail, ripping it off as he ran inside. Writhing in pain, Digger had managed to reach his front feet out and pull his severed tail inside.

Outside, the beast screamed with rage, lunging at the small entrance to Digger's den, snapping its giant teeth.

176

Finally, it stomped away with footsteps that shook the ground. Digger had stayed in the cave until hunger drove him outside. Then he ate until he couldn't hold another root or leaf.

The small dinosaur roused himself from the memory, shuddering, and set off again.

They came now to a rocky hill, and a strange alertness ran through Digger. He could feel it: bone calling to bone.

"What is it, Digger?" asked Puck. "What are ye thinking?"

Digger trembled with excitement. He could sense his cave, and his tail inside. He began digging furiously.

"Look at ye go!" cried Puck. "What a digger ye be, Digger!" The sprite hopped off Digger's back and turned a somersault, then did a little dance on a large toadstool.

Mud and pebbles flew into the air as Digger dug deeper and deeper. At last he came to the mouth of the cave. Stooping, he padded in, followed by Puck.

There, in a heap, lay the bones of his beautiful tail! Carefully Digger dug a long space around them and laid the bones in an orderly row.

Puck lifted his brows. "That's a tail for a tale," he said. He snapped his fingers over the bones and sang again, three times:

"Grow you muscle, skin and scale;

Tonight we found a missing tail."

The bones indeed became covered with muscle, skin and scale. With another finger snap, Puck attached the purple tail to Digger's stump. The dinosaur gave a scream of delight that echoed all through the cave. He ran out of the cave. He hopped up and down. He whisked his tail from side to side. He ran in circles of happiness. He threw his head back and shrieked at the moon—which, he noticed, was much lower in the sky.

"We must get back before dawn," said Puck, following his glance. "Best be on our way." Hopping again on Digger's back, he commanded, "Run."

Digger ran lickety-split for the city. How thrilling to feel his long tail waving behind him as he passed brambles and trees, villages, and always the winding river.   Soon they were on the cobbled streets of London, and then Digger was running up the grand stone steps of the museum.

Puck mumbled his chant. The huge doors opened and closed. Digger clickety-clicked along the great hall, past the sperm whale, down the corridor and hallway, until he came to the little gallery with his plinth.

"Up ye go," said the sprite and he snapped his fingers to make Digger visible again as the dinosaur hopped onto the box-like table. The dinosaur's tail hung over the edge and trailed on the floor.

"We must make a grand show of this marvel," said Puck. Carefully he lifted the tail, curled it around Digger's upright body, and draped the end over one of Digger's arms.

Dawn broke. For a moment, the dinosaur stood holding the end of his purple tail. Then scales, skin, and muscle all faded away. Digger was a skeleton again.

Puck remained invisible, waiting to see what would happen.

Just before opening hours, the museum warder came along on his rounds. His hands were clasped behind his back, and he was whistling as he strolled through the doorway.

"How's our little Dinosaurus Fossurus sine Cauda?" he said, then stopped. His jaw dropped. He came closer to the plinth, holding out a shaking hand to touch the bony tail.

"How can this be?" he whispered hoarsely. Grabbing his hair with both hands, he shouted, "It can't be!" and dashed out the door.

Puck's laughter twittered against the walls of the small gallery. He turned three somersaults before he could catch his breath. He glanced at the plinth, and it seemed to him that if skeletons could smile, Digger was grinning.

179

The warder returned, this time with the director, Mr. William Henry Flower.

Mr. Flower walked around the skeleton, examining it carefully. He ran his hand along the skeleton's spine and tail. He read the information card, frowned, and tapped a forefinger against his lower lip. Then he cleared his throat.

"We shall have to change the label," he said, as if nothing unusual had happened. "Dinosaurus Fossurus cum Cauda Longa."

"Long-tailed Digger Dinosaur, of course," the warder agreed. He licked his lips. "But how . . .?"

"Come back with me to the office," said Mr. Flower. "We must have a proper card made immediately." He strode out the door, followed by the warder, who gave the skeleton one last distressed glance over his shoulder.

Puck doubled over from new laughter. When he calmed down again, he hopped onto the plinth and from there to the dinosaur's bony back. Putting his head close to Digger's, he whispered,

"Well, my friend, I've had my fun.

Now it's late and I must run.

"Enjoy your tail," he added, as he leaped to the floor.

Sparkles of thanks and happiness floated from the skeleton, so strong they stirred something new in Puck's mischievous chest. His deeds were not the kind that usually brought gratitude—that wasn't the purpose of mischief. An odd pleasure washed through him as he ambled down the corridor to the great hall and out into the warm morning.

"Gratitude," he muttered to a pigeon, as he skipped down the wide stone steps. "Can't have too much of that! It'll spoil my reputation."

But he couldn't shake the sense of satisfaction it gave him, as he looked around for a crow, ready to start the long flight home.

The Swan Cape

Watching the snowy swans as they swam Raisa muttered, "Why should they have what I can't have?"

Once upon a Russian lake in Count Timurov's forest, there lived two swans, Sonya and Stefan. They were husband and wife and devoted to each other. A Rusalka named Raisa envied them their love. Watching the snowy swans as they swam or ate pondweed, she muttered, "Why should they have what I can't have?"

One day, watching the swans paddle among reeds at the lake edge, the water spirit decided to punish their happiness. Her green eyes glittered. She thrashed her scaly tail, pointing two pale fingers at Sonya. In a flash, Sonya became a beautiful maiden wearing a long cape of white swan feathers. Looking down at herself, Sonya shrieked.

In shock, Stefan eyed the woman with pale wavy hair who had replaced his wife. "Sonya," he cried, "can this be you?"

"Stefan, I'm lost to you!"

185

The air rang with Raisa's shrill laughter.

The Firebird, the protector of goodness, had seen everything from her perch on a birch tree branch. She flew to Sonya's shoulder, her red and golden feathers gleaming. "I cannot undo Raisa's spell," she warbled, "but I can change it."

Fluttering her wings over Sonya's head, she said, "Go into the count's forest. A woodcutter and his wife live there in a small hut. Stay and help them. In three years, at the stroke of midnight, you'll become a swan again. But," warned the Firebird, "never lose your swan cape, or you'll remain human."

Weeping, Sonya kissed Stefan's beak and set off. The Firebird stayed to comfort him.

In the middle of the lake, Raisa gnashed her teeth, pulling out strands of her long green hair. They must not be reunited, she thought. If only I could steal that cape! But her fish tail kept her from going on land.

The woodcutter and his wife were deeply concerned when Sonya appeared at their door. "I've lost my home," she told them, her face still wet with tears.

"Stay with us," offered the wife. To her husband, she whispered, "The poor girl is in shock." They gave Sonya a pallet to sleep on. As weeks passed, the wife taught Sonya to spin and weave. Sonya drew water from the well and

186

cooked for the old couple, though she only ate pondweed herself. In time, they came to love her like a daughter.

By day Sonya wore the feathered cape. At night, she kept it under her pillow. Each evening when work was done, she walked to the lake, calling Stefan. Then they sat under the birch tree, dreaming of the day the spell would end.

In the center of the lake, Raisa watched and waited.

One afternoon, in the third year of the spell, Count Timurov galloped through his vast estate. He slowed to a canter and straightened the riding jacket over his silk tunic. He grinned and thought, My castle; my village; my forest; my good looks. I have much to offer a wife. I will marry a princess!

The horse cantered to the forest edge, then to the lake beyond. Timurov spied Stefan. What a beautiful swan, he mused.

Raisa swam near, her heart roiling with new plans. She pointed two fingers at the horse, then the count. The horse turned and galloped toward the woodcutter's hut.

"What's got into you!" exclaimed Timurov; but he let the horse have its way.

At the hut, Sonya was drawing water from the well. Seeing her slim neck, her pale wavy hair, and her dark mysterious eyes, Timurov forgot about the princess. This beautiful maiden must be mine, he thought.

Dismounting his horse, he strode into the hut, the heels of his boots echoing against the wooden floor. "Is that your daughter outside?" he demanded.

The woodcutter bowed. "Sire," he said, "she is a foundling. Is there some offense?"

Just then Sonya came through the door.

The count smiled. "I mean to marry this maiden."

Sonya gasped. "I cannot marry you!"

Timurov's smile vanished. "My carriage will come for you next week," he snapped. He gave the old couple a look of warning and left.

The woodcutter shivered. "The count owns everything," he told Sonya.

"He will punish us if you refuse," said his wife.

Frightened, Sonya ran to the lake edge and told Stefan what had happened.

Thinking over the old couple's words, Stefan finally said, "If he will punish them, he will also punish you if you refuse. I'll follow you and watch over you until the three years are over."

The Firebird fluttered from her branch on the birch tree to Sonya's shoulder. "I too will follow and protect you both," she warbled.

From the water, Raisa muttered, "So you think." She dived down deep and swam through underground streams to the lake by the castle.

A week later, a gold wedding carriage, encrusted with rubies and emeralds, arrived at the woodcutter's hut. Tearfully Sonya said goodbye to the old couple. All the way to the castle, she stared out the window. The sight of Stefan flying above and the brilliant Firebird behind him gave her courage.

For three days, Count Timurov's cooks created special dishes. Sonya ate nothing. Musicians sang. Sonya wouldn't smile. She refused silk gowns, wearing only her homespun dress and her snowy swan cape. Each night she closed her chamber door and wept. The Firebird perched on the windowsill to comfort her. Each morning Sonya walked the path to the lake below the courtyard to visit Stefan. The Firebird perched in a nearby apple tree.

On the fourth morning, Timurov strode down to the water's edge and found Sonya sitting on a stone bench, watching a swan. He frowned. When had he gotten this swan? How peaceful Sonya's face looked! Jealousy curdled his heart.

"You have eyes for a swan but not for your own husband?" he shouted. "I give you fine clothes, yet you wear

189

that feathered cape? I have made you a countess, and you show no gratitude?"

"You married me against my will."

"It is an honor to marry a count," Timurov fumed. "I command you to be happy!" He wheeled and stormed back to the castle.

In the center of the lake, Raisa smiled.

The Firebird fluttered to a window in the castle dining hall. The count sat alone, picking at his breakfast. Making herself invisible, the Firebird flew close to him and planted a needle of love in his heart. As pain pricked his chest, Timurov thought of Sonya. She hadn't eaten since coming to the castle.

Slowly he rose and returned to the lake's edge, where Sonya sat sobbing.

"If I let you keep this swan for a pet," he said, "will you eat something?"

Sonya looked up. "My lord, I only eat pondweed."

"Pondweed!" Timurov ran his hand over his dark curly beard, then cleared his throat. "The cooks will prepare pondweed delicacies for you from now on," he promised.

After that, Sonya became friendlier. She took her meals with him. She even smiled. Although it troubled Timurov to see her still wear the swan cape, the needle of love worked even deeper into his heart. He began to think of other ways to make her happy.

"Would you like a shelter over your bench when you sit by the lake?" he asked. "It will shade you from sun and keep you dry from the rain." Sonya clapped her hands with joy. Next, he had a jeweled feeding dish made for her swan. Soon he was walking down to the lake each morning to feed the swan himself, before Sonya awoke.

"What else would she like?" he wondered. "Ah! I'll move the woodcutter and his wife to the castle." He rode out to the hut and made his offer.

"Sire, we wouldn't know how to act in a castle," said the woodcutter.

"We are happy where we are," agreed his wife.

"There must be something I can do for you," Timurov insisted.

"If I had some help cutting and stacking wood . . ." said the woodcutter.

"If we could visit Sonya sometimes . . ." said his wife.

From then on, a servant went every day to their hut to cut and stack wood. Each week a carriage brought the couple to the castle to visit Sonya for one night. The sight of their glowing faces gave Timurov a strange contentment.

He began complimenting the cooks for the dishes they created. "Prepare treats for yourself," he ordered. The clothiers were given fine sashes and belts. Everyone noticed how the count had changed.

Raisa noticed too. Rage frazzled her green hair. It wasn't fair for everyone to be so happy. I must get that cape, I must! she thought. If she didn't, when the spell ended, Sonya would be a swan again and be reunited with Stefan.

One morning, before dawn, Raisa woke with a new idea. The third year was one day short of ending. I can't steal the cape, she thought, but the count can.

She swam to the reeds at the lake edge. A few feet away, Stefan still slept. Raisa pointed her pale fingers to make him sleep a little longer, looking carefully around for the Firebird. But the Firebird was with Sonya.

When Timurov came to fill Stefan's dish with pondweed, Raisa rose from the water, balancing on her tail. She beckoned him to come close. Slowly he approached, trying not to tremble before her ghostly figure. "Your countess is a sorceress," Raisa hissed. "Do you not wonder why she keeps that feathered cape near her?"

Timurov looked quickly away. He had tried not to wonder.

"The cape is evil," she warned. "A wicked spell was chanted into each feather."

"It's only a cape," Timurov protested. But, he thought to himself, a spirit would know things I don't know.

"The countess is biding her time," said Raisa. "She wants to take over your castle and destroy you." Knowing that fear is a powerful friend of evil, Raisa threw a needle of fear into the count's heart. It landed next to the Firebird's needle of love.

"Bring me the cape, tonight, before it's too late," Raisa whispered, and sank into the water.

Love and fear struggled inside the count's heart: "The countess is gentle," he mused. "The servants love her! Her smiles make me happy." Then he wondered, "Why won't she part with the cape? Why does she eat pondweed? Is she a sorceress?"

Night came. The maids bathed Sonya and saw her to bed. Timurov waited in the hallway. When all was quiet, he stole into her bedchamber and tiptoed to her bedside.

Sonya smiled in her sleep, dreaming she was a swan again. A pang shot through Timurov's heart as he reached under the pillow and eased the cape out. Barely breathing, he sneaked out, slipping along the corridor and down to the front door.

The Firebird saw him and followed.

Outside, Timurov went down the great stone stairs, crossed the courtyard, and trod the path to the lake. How fortunate I was warned, he thought. How foolish I've been. Yet his heart ached with each step. Halfway down the path, he paused and held the cape up in the moonlight. The glossy feathers shimmered.

The Firebird flew close, hovering before him. "Do not destroy the cape," she warbled.

Frightened by this feathered creature with a woman's face, Timurov gasped, "The cape is evil. And you must be too!"

"It is not evil. Let love conquer fear," she urged.

The count turned away and hastened down the path. But, as the Firebird flew back to the castle, her words floated on the night breeze.

It is not good to destroy things, Timurov thought. If the cape is evil, I can protect the countess by burying it. He dug a hole under the roots of an oak tree, stuffed the cape inside, and hurried back to the castle.

At sunrise, Sonya awoke and reached under her pillow, then screamed. She flung the pillow aside. All the maids came running.

The count came to her door. "What's wrong?" he asked, avoiding her eyes.

"My cape!" Sonya cried. "I must have it!" Her wails carried all the way to the lake, where Raisa swam around in gleeful circles.

Servants looked throughout the castle, trying to find the cape. Timurov pretended to look, too. All morning the search went on. In the dining hall, chairs were up-ended. Cupboard doors hung open. Sonya was too grieved to eat her mid-day meal. She sat at the long table, her face in her hands. Unable to bear her misery, Timurov hurried to his chamber.

The Firebird followed and flew to his shoulder, warbling, "You must correct what you have done."

Timurov gulped. "I have saved my wife from wickedness," he managed to say.

"You are causing her much sorrow."

The needle of fear pricked the count's heart. Grimacing from pain, he said, "I was warned the cape is evil."

"You were misled. Only the cape can save your wife from suffering." The Firebird leaned closer and whispered, "Let love conquer fear."

The needle of love she had planted earlier moved within him. Instead of a sharp sting, he felt a gentle memory of his wife's happiness. Overcome with remorse, he ran downstairs and outside. He dashed along the path to the oak tree and dug out the cape. Shaking the dirt from its feathers, he rushed back to the castle and into the dining hall. "I found your cape," he gasped.

Sonya snatched it and threw it over her shoulders. Tears of joy ran down her face.

A weight dropped from Timurov's heart. "Prepare a feast, to celebrate," he ordered the cooks. When they were gone, he turned to Sonya, ashamed. "It was I who took your cape," he confessed.

Sonya looked at him for a long moment. "I forgive you," she said, quietly. Then she asked, "May we have our feast late tonight? When the clock strikes twelve, all that has confused you will become clear."

Late that night the dining table was laid with silver bowls, jeweled plates and golden goblets that caught the candlelight. The count and his courtiers dined on herb soup, sole filet, baked ham, and small roasted potatoes, followed by fruit and shortbread topped with cream. As usual, Sonya ate pondweed. The last of the gleaming dishes were cleared away just as the tall clock near the door began striking midnight.

Sonya rose and walked to the doorway, her white cape gleaming. She inclined her head to the count, saying, "My lord, I take my leave." A moment later, the twelfth stroke sounded, and Sonya disappeared. In her place stood a beautiful white swan.

Cries of surprise ran around the dining hall. The Firebird fluttered to the Count's shoulder. "This is why the countess couldn't love you," she said softly. "An evil Rusalka cast a spell on her. All this time she has been true to her real husband, the swan who swims in your lake."

Count Timurov heaved a deep sigh of loneliness. As he did so, the needle of fear fell out of his heart. The needle of love went even deeper, and he forgot his own sorrow, thinking of Sonya's instead. "I must return her to her true husband," he said.

He and Sonya led a procession to the lake. Above them, the Firebird spread her bright wings. When they reached the water's edge, Sonya paused. In the moon's silver light, Stefan swam toward her. She leaped into the water to meet him.

"From this day," Count Timurov vowed, "these noble swans are under my protection."

The Firebird perched on Timurov's shoulder, her wings shimmering. "I will remain to protect you all," she warbled.

"Good count," she added. "There is a maiden in your village you might love. She is not royally born, but she has a true and noble heart."

Thinking of the woodcutter and his wife, he asked, "Could she be happy in a castle?"

"Count Timurov," replied the Firebird. "Now that love has shaped your heart, you have more than a castle to offer a wife."

Thus, Timurov found a wife who loved him, and Stefan and Sonya lived long, happy lives under their care. By day, the swans swam side-by-side, gliding across the water. At evening, they floated under the rising moon. Often, they turned to each other, their long necks curving, their beaks touching, happy to be together again.

As for Raisa . . . The Rusalka returned to the lake by the forest, where she haunts it to this very day.

The Carnival

The animals flowed in the melody's stream—the magical notes of a musical dream.

O nce upon a Mardi Gras, Camille Saint-Saëns was pleased. His musical fantasy was finished. Eleven friends had copies of the score. They entered his Paris salon, one by one, and tuned their instruments: a clarinet, a piccolo, two violins, a viola, a cello, a double bass, a xylophone, and a glockenspiel. Noel and Jolie, all grown up, sat at the piano.

Camille waved his baton. "You must dream the music you play," he said, "for this is a fantasy." And so began the Carnival, with piano trills and strings.

Slowly music filled the room. Musical notes leaped off the score and began to circle above. They turned to ribbons of music that stretched into a glittering path. The day was warm, the window raised. The path rose high and floated out, swept in the March breeze.

The ribbons stretched wide, and soon became a colorful rainbow of sound: Silver and gold; red, orange, and yellow, every shade of green. Turquoise blue, a purple hue, and colors few have seen. Unrolling there; fluttering here; a colorful path in every sphere, all woven from music that sent out a call: "Come to the Carnival."

In Bouconne Forest a fearless lion mounted a golden strand.

The kangaroos gave mighty leaps to a gleaming copper arch.

A pearlescent path led to Backmuir Wood, and a unicorn hopped on.

An amber road unrolled before a tortoise who could dance.

Hens and cocks fluffed feathers and trod a velvety green strip.

The dinosaur ran as fast as he could on a glowing purple band.

Nerina swam with her newfound friends in a magic silver stream.

The cuckoo flew to a ruby path that matched his glowing heart.

The peacock stepped on an arc of blue; the swans swam a diamond beam.

As the music swirled, and the animals twirled on their way to the carnival, it was plain to see, in this jamboree, they were sadly out of order.

Elroi shook his lion's mane. "I see I must take charge: Get in line, all of you, and I will lead the march."

The hens all clucked. The roosters crowed. They filed behind the lion.

"Now me," said Omar, the unicorn, prancing and shaking his milky horn.

Trinette was next. She danced into place and slowly tried to bow.

Angelique followed, telling herself, "If Pierre could see me now!"

Minkie and Jilli, Bakana too, leaped into line, roo after roo.

Nerina floated behind them with her friends from the Trocadéro.

'Tulio, it's our turn," Dulce said. "Please get in line, my hero."

Next in line little Eldwin flew. "New friends!" he cried. "Cuckoo, cuckoo."

Pakrit fell in, his tail spread wide. Once more he swelled with peacock pride.

Jolie and Noel, the grown-up twins, played their scales with secretive grins, as the cello thrummed, and the violin hummed, "Come to the Carnival!"

"Come to the Carnival!"

Digger the dinosaur followed Pakrit, happy his tail now was complete.

Sonya, the swan, and Stefan, her love, swam at the end, both floating above.

Camille Saint-Saëns paused. "I hear them coming!" he said. He wildly waved his baton.

"We must give them room, we must make some space. Play on, play on. We must stretch this place. They are outside the window now!"

The music grew louder. The colors glowed brighter. The melodies rose to the salon's ceiling, which floated away from so much feeling. And all to make room for the animals who came to the carnival.

One by one they crossed the sill. Round and round the animals marched. On glittering ribbons of color, they traipsed round the musicians' heads: They stomped and they fluttered or ran like the wind. They danced like shrubs or waved a trunk. They bounded in glee or swam or brayed, happy to be in this grand parade. Flapping their wings or fanning a tail, rattling bones or floating in grace, the animals flowed in the melody's stream—the magical notes of a musical dream.

And then:

The sun went down. Camille's baton slowed. The musicians yawned. The music stopped.

In silence, the ribbons of color unwound, taking the animals home.

On the evening breeze, over shadowy trees, the animals floated home.

The carnival was over.

Acknowledgements and Sources

I want to express my deep appreciation for those who read earlier versions of these stories and gave feedback. Their suggestions were always helpful and made the collection stronger. Special thanks go to Marilyn Mazzocco's 2nd grade class at Elder Creek Elementary School and Don Brown's split 4th/5th grade class at Peter Burnett Elementary School, both in Sacramento, CA in spring of 2008. Additional thanks go to Louise Munro Foley, Kathleen Garrison and David Wood, and my super beta readers, Nancy Herman, Susan Britton, Rosi Hollinbeck, Randall Buechner, Jennifer Hanson, JaNay Brown-Wood, Patricia Lawton, for invaluable critiques.

Many thanks to Lynda Staker, Australian lecturer and author of *The Complete Guide to The Care of Macropods,* and the two-volume *Macropod Husbandry, Healthcare & Medicinal*, for her advice about the Australian red kangaroo and its habitat. Thanks, also, to James Hatton, Archives and Records Assistant at The Natural History Museum in London, who advised me on how dinosaur skeletons would have been displayed and labeled and who was superintendent of the museum at the time of Digger's story, and to Ms. Simone Wells, Enquiries Officer, Dept. of Paleontology, The Natural History Museum, London, for information about dinosaurs that might have existed in prehistoric England, and to Beverly Meyer, for Latin translations.

For Angelique's story, I read (and cried through) *Jumbo: This Being the True Story of the Greatest Elephant in the World*, by Paul Chambers, and *Modoc: The True Story of the Greatest Elephant That Ever Lived*, by Ralph Helfer. For the burro Tulio's story, I read a truly humorous translation of Cervantes' *Don Quixote*. Thanks go to Dr. Wolfgang Kneller and his wife, Mariana, for their information about Germany's Black Forest and cuckoo clocks. I also had the good fortune to visit the Jardin des Plantes and the Trocadéro in Paris to firm up descriptions in Angelique's story and Nerina's story. For further research, I consulted too many sites to list, learning about the Malabar thrush, the Mediterranean tortoise, onagers (wild donkeys), piano duets for 19th century children, traveling menageries, legendary magic figures, etc. What I have written in this collection is distilled imagination of what is possible in fantasy/fairytales.

Last, but not least, my deepest thanks to Liz and Ernie Pucci for connecting me with such fine illustrators, Susan and Peter Fraser, and to Belanger Books for the opportunity to share this collection with other readers, young and old alike.

The Music Behind the Stories

There are many biographies online of the French composer, Camille Saint-Saëns (1835-1921). This page is only a light sketch dealing with Saint-Saëns' composition, *The Carnival of the Animals,* the inspiration for this collection of stories

Saint-Saëns' work in many genres includes the famous symphonic poem, "Danse Macabre" and the opera, *Samson et Dalila.*[1] In 1886, Saint-Saëns wrote *The Carnival of Animals*, a "humorous fantasy".[2] There are fourteen sections, one for each animal, and a "finale".

While taking a break from work on a symphony during a vacation in Austria, Saint-Saëns wrote this humorous fantasy purely for fun.[3] However, according to Hailey Colwell,[4] Saint-Saëns was so

[1] Cummings, Robert. "Camille Saint-Saëns | Biography & History." *AllMusic*, AllMusic, www.allmusic.com/artist/camille-saint-saëns-mn0000688311/biography.

[2] Britannica, The Editors of Encyclopaedia. "Camille Saint-Saëns." *Encyclopædia Britannica*, Encyclopædia Britannica, Inc., 24 Apr. 2017, www.britannica.com/biography/Camille-Saint-Saens.

[3] Automatisering, Roffel. "Saint-Saëns - Carnival of the Animals: Description -- Classic Cat." *Classic Cat - the Free Classical Music Directory*, Classic Cat - the Free Classical Music Directory, 2016, www.classiccat.net/saint-saens_c/_cota.info.php.

fearful it would damage his reputation as a serious composer, he would only permit it to be played in private, except for the cello piece, "The Swan". Colwell goes on to explain each movement, what it portrays, and how it conveys the particular animal involved. It is my hope that these stories capture the humor and fun of Saint-Saëns' music.

---

[4] Colwell, Hailey. "'Carnival of the Animals': Inside Saint-Saens's Children's Classic | Your Classical | YourClassical." *Star Wars Music: What Were John Williams's Classical Influences? | Your Classical | YourClassical*, American Public Media, 29 June 2015, www.yourclassical.org/story/2015/06/29/carnival-of-the-animals-saint-saens.

About the Author

Elizabeth Varadan is a former elementary teacher who has always loved music, art, and other cultures. She and her husband live in Sacramento, California, but travel frequently to Spain. Her children's fiction has appeared in *Story Friends*, *Ladybug*, and *Skipping Stones Magazine*, as well as in the 2016 anthology, *Beyond Watson* (Belanger Books). Her middle-grade mystery featuring Sherlock Holmes, *Imogene and the Case of the Missing Pearls* (MX Publishing), was published in 2015. Her picture book, *Dragonella*, was published by Belanger Books in 2017 (English edition) and in 2018 (Spanish edition).

You can visit her at her blogs:

http://elizabethvaradansfourthwish.blogspot.com

http://victorianscribbles.blogsspot.com

or at her author page at Amazon:

https://www.amazon.com/Elizabeth-Varadan/e/B003VOTCFG

Belanger Books

Made in the USA
Columbia, SC
20 December 2018